m

★ ★ ★ ★ ★

Armadillos

& OLD LACE

KINKY FRIEDMAN

★ ★ ★ ★ ★

SIMON &

SCHUSTER

New York

London

Toronto

Sydney

Tokyo

Singapore

SIMON & SCHUSTER
Rockefeller Center
1230 Avenue of the Americas
New York, New York 10020

This book is a work of fiction. Names, characters, places and
incidents are either products of the author's imagination or are used
fictitiously. Any resemblance to actual events or locales or persons,
living or dead, is entirely coincidental.

SIMON & SCHUSTER and colophon are registered trademarks of
Simon & Schuster Inc.
Designed by Pei Loi Koay
Manufactured in the United States of America

1   3   5   7   9   10   8   6   4   2

Library of Congress Cataloging-in-Publication Data

Friedman, Kinky.
Armadillos & old lace/Kinky Friedman.
p.   cm.
1. Private investigators—Texas—Fiction. I. Title.
II. Title: Armadillos and old lace.
PS3556.R527A89   1994
813'.54—dc20   94-9811
CIP

ISBN: 0-671-86923-X

This book is dedicated
with lots of love
to

Lottie Cotton

There were ten pretty girls
in the village school
There were ten pretty girls
in the village school
Some were short, some were tall
And the boy loved them all
But you can't marry ten pretty girls.

—TRADITIONAL TEXAS FOLK DANCE

Chapter

★ ★ ★ ★ ★

It was my last night in New York before saddling up the cat, grabbing my old guitar, and heading back to the family ranch in Texas for the summer. Every spring, just about the time I heard my suitcase snap, I vowed never to return to the city. Every fall, I seemed to find myself, almost inexplicably, back in the Big Apple. Sooner or later I was going to have to decide whether Texas or New York was truly my home. Then, in that quiet moment of reflection, I'd hopefully find the answer to the grand and troubling question that has haunted mankind through the ages: What is it that I really want out of life—horsemanure or pigeon shit?

Some of the boys had planned a little send-off at one of my favorite places, Big Wong's on Mott Street in Chinatown. We were sitting at a large round table close enough to the kitchen to hear the cook whistling something from the Hong Kong Hit Parade. McGovern, large Irish society columnist for the *Daily News* and master of the magical background check, had brought about fourteen cases of beer over in paper bags

from the little grocery store across the street. Ratso, my flam-
boyant, flea-market friend, editor of *National Lampoon,* and
somewhat weatherbeaten Dr. Watson, had been quite dis-
heartened when the waiter had told him: "No more roast
pork."

"No more roast pork," Ratso was muttering to himself.
The place closed at ten o'clock and we were pushing that
now.

"It's hard to keep continental dining hours at Big Wong's,"
said McGovern. "You get here after eight o'clock, you're
pretty well hosed."

Rambam, a private investigator who'd worked with me on
some of my cases and was wanted in every state that began
with an "I," stared stonily at the far wall and drank his beer.
The few other guests had already left us with their bottles and
the bill. At the next table, the waiters and busboys, dressed
entirely in white, were silently shoveling down whatever'd
been left over in the kitchen. Their outfits lent a nice institutional touch to the evening. It was a quiet affair.

I could use a little quiet, I reflected. I'd become somewhat
ambivalent about performing country music gigs lately and
I'd come to realize that anyone who uses the word "ambivalent" probably shouldn't have been a country singer in the
first place. Going on the road as a musician was always a
killer, but these days, for me, even staying home could be
murder.

Over the past few years I'd tried my fine Hebrew hand as an
amateur detective in the city, resulting in both the criminals
and the policemen not being my friends. I was an equal opportunity offender.

Worse, the crime-solving lifestyle had brought into my life a myriad of death, destruction, heartbreak, scandal, and a remorseless, lingering, spirit-sucking ennui, though several of the cases were not without charm. In my most recent adventure, which McGovern had dubbed *The Case of Elvis, Jesus & Coca-Cola*, I'd endeavored to locate a missing film about Elvis impersonators directed by my friend Tom Baker, who'd recently gone to Jesus himself. Because of that case I'd lost one or two girlfriends, depending on how you looked at it.

I glanced at my partners in crime seated around the table and wondered if they realized how much *Elvis, Jesus & Coca-Cola* had taken out of me. When I left New York this time, I figured, I might really never return. At least not until Jesus got his own postage stamp.

"You've never held a real job as long as I've known you," Rambam was saying. "What makes you think you need a vacation?"

"It's not a vacation," I said, quoting my sister Marcie. "It's a lifestyle."

"The Kinkstah works," said Ratso, rising above the roast pork situation to come to my defense. "He's just finished a very grueling tour. Hey, I wonder if they have any pork gruel?"

"Believe me," I said, "opening for Henny Youngman at a sports bar in New Jersey on Mother's Day is hard work. I got so hammered after the show from being subjected to seven hundred video screens that I walked on my knuckles into a wall and smashed my guitar."

"What a shame," said Rambam. "It's an omen. God wants you to go out and get a real job."

"So you can be like the rest of us miserable bastards," said McGovern. He laughed a loud, hearty, Irish laugh that seemed to echo in the little room. Several of our neighboring diners looked over briefly from their fish head soup.

"Why is it," said Ratso, "that the kitchen help always gets better food than we do?"

"Racism," said McGovern.

As Ratso began his uncanny shell game of putting money into and taking it out of a pot to pay the check, I sat back and looked around the table. McGovern, Ratso, and Rambam, while very different in style and substance, were all New York down to the core of the Big Apple. There weren't many like them in the Texas Hill Country. We liked to keep it that way.

"Are you taking the cat?" McGovern asked. Ratso palmed a twenty from the middle of the table and replaced it with a five.

"Of course," I said. "Last year I left the cat with Winnie and by the time I came back she'd turned her into a strident feminist." Winnie Katz ran a lesbian dance class in the loft above mine.

"It's not the first pussy Winnie's gotten her hands on," said Rambam.

The cat would like Texas, I figured. She'd live on a beautiful ranch in a little green valley surrounded by hills. There'd be oak and cottonwood and cedar trees, streams flowing by, and lizards to chase on every rock. There'd be the spiritual elbow room available that you'd never find in the city. The freedom just to be a cat. She'd like it, all right. Of course, the cat would like an exhibit of twelfth-century Portuguese architecture if you put a can of tuna in front of it.

As we left Big Wong's and walked up Mott Street that night, I could almost feel the hot Texas sun on my shoulders and the gentle breeze rustling the sycamore against my old green trailer like the wings of a cowboy angel. In the skies over Manhattan the stars were barely bright enough to make a wish on. I'd wait until I got to Texas.

"The thing I like about the Chinese," said Ratso, as he looked around the crowded, oblivious street, "is that they don't hold the Jews responsible for killing Jesus."

"Yeah," said Rambam, "but I think they know we contracted the lumber."

Being in the process of lighting up and concomitantly attempting to laugh, I came precariously close to swallowing my cigar. I wondered fleetingly if there was a form of the Heimlich maneuver available for Americans who swallowed their cigars while laughing. Most likely not, I reasoned. There weren't that many people who actually smoked cigars and, for those who did, life, very probably, was not all that funny. You could always not smoke and not laugh. Then you'd probably get run over by a bookmobile.

There is, of course, a very thin line between laughing and choking to death. Both sound about the same, look about the same, and, often, may feel quite similar to the occupant. The only difference is that if you're only laughing you'll eventually stop, but if you're truly choking to death, you'll go on laughing forever.

Apparently, I was only laughing. I said good-bye to my three companions as we dodged traffic on Canal Street. McGovern gave me a bear hug and Rambam clasped my shoulder with an iron grip. Ratso shook hands and copped a cigar from me. Then he borrowed my butt-cutter. Then he bummed a light.

"I'm a full-service friend," I said.

"Well, at least you'll get some rest down there, Kinkstah," said Ratso. "Nothing much happens in Texas."

"That's true," I said. "We've got a lot of wide open spaces."

"Especially between people's ears," said Ratso.

2

★ ★ ★ ★ ★

The next morning as the plane dipped like a Spanish dancer over the New York skyline, I watched the twin Trade Towers shrink to the Tinkertoys of a child, and the Statue of Liberty to the bright prize from a Cracker Jack box. Somewhere below, McGovern was probably still sleeping, dreaming of old-fashioned silk skirts rustling across make-believe ballrooms.

Ratso was down there too, someplace. Most likely tossing and turning in his cluttered warehouse of an apartment, having a nightmare about the five hundred interviews he'd soon be embarking upon in order to complete his new book on Abbie Hoffman. Abbie was down there, too, I reflected. At peace finally. Somewhere off to the left.

Rambam, no doubt, had been up all night on a stake-out. Right now he was probably sipping coffee in a parked car and watching a door or a window or an alleyway. Those are good things to watch because, unlike many aspects of human experience, something meaningful may occasionally come out of them.

The cat had never taken kindly to the notion of leaving the loft on Vandam Street where the two of us had survived more winters than the saber-toothed tiger. Like many New Yorkers, the cat believed that no life whatsoever existed outside the confines of Manhattan. I could just imagine what her mental state would be like after flying four hours in the baggage compartment in a cage next to a golden retriever and somebody's pet boa constrictor. I'd given her half a cat Valium before we'd left. The other half I'd taken myself. If mine didn't kick in soon, I figured, I might have to up-grade to heroin suppositories.

I watched New York telescope away and then disappear completely beneath the cloud cover. I thought of the troubles and tension conventions I was leaving behind. The friends. The lovers. The little black puppet head sitting all alone on top of the refrigerator. How many times, with the colorful parachute attached and the key to the building wedged in its mouth, had I thrown it out the window into the eager hands of visitors and housepests? How many times had it come back to me, still smiling one of the most genuine smiles in New York City? What the hell, I thought. Maybe I'd get a little head in Texas.

I sipped a Bloody Mary for a while, then I closed my eyes and drifted through time and space like campfire smoke. We weren't anywhere near Texas yet, but I could already see the ranch. My folks had bought the place forty years ago and in the summertime they'd operated it as a camp for boys and girls. I'd been a camper there myself, then a counselor, running the waterfront. These days, however, I felt a bit o-l-d to interact too intensely with the kids. The range of my responsibilities now rambled from dropping the laundry in town every morning in the pickup truck, to poisoning occasional mounds of fire ants, to feeding the hummingbirds, to singing a song once in a while at a campfire or hoedown. It was strenuous work.

The ranch was called Echo Hill. I had nothing but happy memories from all the years I'd been involved with the place. Now, for the first time, like echoes in a dream, I had a slight sense of foreboding about my imminent return to the Hill Country. A half-conscious uneasiness that I attributed to the fact that the guy sitting next to me in the plane looked like a mad scientist from Pakistan. If I'd known then what was awaiting me in Texas, I'd have grabbed the pilot by the beezer and told him to turn the plane around.

I woke from a fitful sleep, and having nodded out through lunch, had to make do with another Bloody Mary and a healthy piece of celery. I needed all the celery I could get. The accumulated stress of living in New York was still weighing heavily upon me. I felt vaguely troubled with a sidecar of impending doom as I looked out over what some New Yorkers call "fly-over country." America, I suppose. The place where celery comes from.

I drew some comfort from an old Texas axiom: Whether your destination is heaven or hell, first you have to change planes in Dallas–Fort Worth.

3

★ ★ ★ ★ ★

It was late in the afternoon when I finally arrived in San Antonio, but the weather was still hotter than a stolen tamale. It reminded me of my days with the Peace Corps working in the jungles of Borneo as an agricultural extension worker. My job had been to distribute seeds upriver to the natives. In two and a half years, however, the Peace Corps never sent me any seeds. In the end, I had to resort to distributing my own seed upriver, which had some rather unpleasant repercussions. But I loved the tropics and seldom complained about the weather in Texas. Without it, no one would ever be able to start a conversation.

I breezed through the corridor to the gate and on into the terminal past straw cowboy hats, belt buckles as big as license plates, happy Hispanic families. At the Dallas–Fort Worth airport, where I'd gotten off the plane briefly to smoke a cigar, the women all had that blond, pinched look halfway between Morgan Fairchild and a praying mantis. The men at DFW appeared to have come in on a wing and a prayer themselves.

They'd looked well fed and fairly smarmy, like so many secular Jimmy Swaggarts. At the San Antonio airport the people looked like real Texans. Even the one Hare Krishna had a nice "Y'all" going for him.

Greyhound bus stations, I reflected as I passed long rows of television chairs all individually tuned to "Ironsides," used to tell you a lot about the character of a town. Today, it's airports. All bus stations tell you anymore is the character of the local characters, and there's damn few of them left these days in most places. I wasn't even sure if I was still one myself.

I waited at the baggage claim for a period of time roughly comparable to the length of the Holy Roman Empire.

"What comes around goes around," I said to a man who was dressed as either a pimp or an Aryan golfer.

"True story," he said. "Last time I went to New Jersey the airline sent all my luggage to Las Vegas."

"Sounds like your toilet kit had more fun than you did," I said.

We waited.

Eventually, with suitcase, guitar, and pet carrier in hand, I strolled onto the sun-blinded San Antonio sidewalk like a lost mariachi and gazed around for anybody wearing an Echo Hill T-shirt. The cat gazed around, too. She had not taken the trip very well, apparently, and at the moment, appeared to be pissed off enough to scratch out the eyes of Texas.

If someone is late to meet you in New York it is cause for major stress and consternation. But Texas is close enough to Mexico to have absorbed by some kind of cultural osmosis a healthy sense of *mañana*. In the old days at the ranch, my brother Roger always used to throw any leftover food on anybody's plate out in the backyard. "Somethin'll git it," he'd say.

In the same way, I knew someone would get me. The cat did not seem to share my confidence. She made loud, baleful noises and scratched unpleasantly at the bars of the cage. Several passersby stopped briefly to stare at us.

"Don't make a scene," I said. "We'll be at the ranch in about an hour."

The cat continued making exaggerated mournful moaning noises and clawing at the cage. The new vice-president of the Nosey Young Women's Society came by and bent down over the pet carrier.

"Is he being mean to you?" she said to the cat. "Did he make you fly in that little cage?"

"We're both on medication," I said. "We've just returned from a little fact-finding trip to Upper Baboon's Asshole."

She left in a vintage 1937 snit.

I took a cigar out of a looped pocket in my lightweight summer hunting vest, began prenuptial arrangements, and, after all preparations were complete, I fired it up with a kitchen match. Always keeping the tip of the cigar well above the flame. I sat down on a cement bench and, for the next ten minutes or so, I watched the wheels go round, as John Lennon would say. Then I got up and stretched my legs a bit until I was almost vivisected by a Dodge Dart. The bumper sticker on the Dodge, I noticed, read: "Not A Well Woman."

Suddenly, there was a horn honking and somebody yelling "Kinkster!" I gazed over and saw a familiar-looking gray pickup with a familiar-looking smiling head sticking out of it. Both the truck and the head were covered with dust. It was Ben Stroud, a counselor at the ranch.

"You came a little early," said Ben.

"That's what she told me last night," I said, as I put the guitar and suitcase in back and the cat in front and climbed in next to Ben, who was drinking a Yoo-Hoo. Ben was not tall but he was large and loud. In Texas, you had to be large and loud. Even if you were an autistic midget. *Especially* if you were an autistic midget.

"What's new at the ranch?" I asked.

"We're still having borientation," said Ben. "The kids don't arrive for a few more days."

I settled back in the cab and entertained a brief vision of the ranchers, as we called them, arriving in a cloud of dust on chartered buses. The old bell in front of the ranch office would be ringing. A small group of counselors, all wearing Echo Hill T-shirts, would be milling about, waiting for their charges in the afternoon sun. Uncle Tom, my dad, would be bringing the buses in, as always, walking in front of them motioning with his arms in the confident, stylish manner of someone leading a cavalry brigade. Uncle Tom would be wearing a light blue pith helmet that looked as if he borrowed it from someone in a Rudyard Kipling story. Tom, who was much loved and respected by the ranchers, counselors, and me, had a great attachment to tradition. It seemed at times that he borrowed himself from a Rudyard Kipling story.

"Tom's assigned me as his Director of External Relations," said Ben. "That means I drop the laundry in town every morning and bring back his paper for him."

"Hey," I said, "that was supposed to be my job! Now I'm an unemployed youth."

"Oh, I don't know about that. You'll be helping me out. I

think you may be plenty busy with other things, too. Pat Knox called Uncle Tom yesterday. She wants to talk to you. It sounds like some pretty mysterious shit."

Pat Knox was the feisty little justice of the peace in Kerr County who'd beaten me for the job some years ago in a hotly contested campaign. One of the other unsuccessful candidates had chopped up his family collie with a hatchet two weeks before the election. He'd still received eight hundred votes.

"What the hell does Pat Knox want?" I said. "Isn't she busy enough marrying people and going around certifying dead bodies?"

"I think that's what she wants to talk to you about."

"Marrying people?"

"No," said Ben. "Dead bodies."

The truck was zimming along headed west on I-10 through the graceful, gently rolling green hills. In the sky ahead of us, backlit by a brilliant, slowly dying sun, we could see an inordinately large number of buzzards circling. They moved methodically, timelessly, as if imbued with ghastly, fateful purpose.

"You'd be crazy to get involved," said Ben.

"Maybe I am crazy," I said. "You know what Carl Jung said: 'Bring me a sane man and I will cure him.'"

"Maybe," said Ben, "Carl Jung will help us with the laundry."

Halfway to Kerrville along I-10 Ben took a left on a smaller road. The cat and I went through periods of dreamtime as we passed a number of small towns on the way to the ranch. Pipe Creek: so named because a local settler over a hundred years ago ran back into his burning cabin to fetch his favorite pipe after an Indian attack. Bandera: "the Cowboy Capital of the World," where Ben and I stopped at the Old Spanish Trail Restaurant and had dinner in the John Wayne Room. The John Wayne Room's sole motif, other than an old covered wagon used as a salad bar and two defunct pinball machines, was fifty-seven photos, pictures, sketches, and sculptures of John Wayne. This thematic approach led to a rather macho orientation among the regulars, and did not serve particularly well as a digestive aid to the occasional traveling butterfly collector from Teaneck, New Jersey.

I had the Mexican Plate and Ben ordered "The Duke," a chicken fried steak approximately the size and appearance of a yellow-and-white-streaked beach umbrella. Many of our fellow diners wore straw cowboy hats and belt buckles the size of license plates. Possibly they were on their way to the San Antonio airport.

By the time we walked out of the O.S.T., dusk was falling over the old western town. We headed up Highway 16 toward Medina. I offered the cat a few residual pieces of "The Duke," but she demurred. We rode to Medina in silence.

Medina was a very small town that had been dying for over a hundred years and actually seemed to almost thrive on that notion. Sometime back in Old Testament days, it had voted not to serve alcoholic beverages. It was open to some debate whether this policy had caused the town's long decline, or whether it had been responsible for eliciting God's favor in enabling the place to die so successfully for so long.

"Stop for a drink?" I said to Ben.

"You kiddin'? I doubt if they'd even let me recycle my Yoo-Hoo."

I thought briefly of what our longtime friend Earl Bucke-lew, who'd lived in the area for over seventy years, once said about the place: "Medina is as dry as a popcorn fart."

"This town is so small," I said to the cat, "that if you blink you won't even see it."

The cat blinked.

Medina wasn't there.

We drove a number of miles farther down 16, then took a left and rolled in a cloud of dust across a cattle guard, down a country road, and into the sunset toward Echo Hill. The ranch was set back about two and a half miles from the scenic little highway, but ever since we passed Pipe Creek we'd been in a world that most New Yorkers never got to see. They believed the deer, the jackrabbits, the raccoons, the sun setting the sky on fire in the west, the cypress trees bathing their knees in the little creek, the pale moon shyly peeking over the mountain—they believed these things only really existed in a Disney movie or a children's storybook. I closed my eyes for a moment, turned a page in my mind. When I opened my eyes again everything was still there. Only New York was gone.

We splashed through a water crossing and two more cattle guards, then turned where the sign said Echo Hill Ranch. Ben drove across a small causeway, then deposited me and the cat and our belongings in front of an antique green trailer that looked like it might've once been the object of a failed time-share arrangement between John Steinbeck and Jack Kerouac. Clearly, it wasn't going anywhere else again, geographically speaking. I felt as much at home as a jet-set gypsy has any right to feel.

I opened the door of the trailer, brushed away a few cobwebs, and turned on a lamp. A happy little raccoon family had apparently been living there over the winter.

"If they want to stay," I said to the cat, "they'll have to pay rent."

The cat said nothing, but it was obvious that she was not amused. In fact, I'd long held a theory that the cat hated every living thing except me. She was ambivalent about me. And that was a nice word for it.

I opened the cage and the cat warily looked out. In a moment she emerged and appeared to gaze in some disgust around the little trailer. It was getting more decrepit every summer, and one of these days even I was going to realize that man can't live on funk alone. The cat stayed a few seconds

KINKY FRIEDMAN

longer, then shot out the open door like a bottle-rocket.

"What'd you expect," I shouted after her. "A condo?"

She'd be back, I thought. Certain cats and certain women always come back. The trouble is that no man is ever quite certain which ones they are.

I lay down on my bunk to take a quick power nap before going up to the lodge to see Tom and say hello to everybody. Ben had said that Tom was having a borientation meeting with the staff in the dining hall. I figured I might do the same for a while here in the trailer. Orient myself to the sound of crickets instead of traffic. Before I closed my eyes I noticed on the far wall that the large framed pictures of Hank Williams and Mahatma Gandhi were still hanging there side by side. They were a little dusty and off-center, but who wasn't that ever did anything great? They stared down at me and I met their cool gaze. Then I closed my eyes for a moment and, from the afterimages of the two faces, little karmic hummingbirds seemed to fly to my pillow.

When I opened my eyes again Hank was smiling at me with that sad spiritually copyrighted crooked smile and Gandhi's eyes were twinkling like the helpless stars above us all. Just before I fell asleep, I recalled, for some reason, what John Lennon had repeatedly asked the Beatles during their meteoric rise to fame: "Did we pass the audition, boys?"

★ ★ ★ 26 ★ ★ ★

Chapter

5

★ ★ ★ ★ ★

I woke up from my power nap to find that the cat had not returned. I put on my boots and headed up to the lodge. Across the nighttime Texas skies someone had unrolled a shimmering blanket of stars. I walked up the little hill toward the lights of the lodge. My father was sitting in an ancient redwood chair on the front lawn, staring into the darkness. He'd made a lot of wishes in seventy years and some of them had come true.

He'd seen thousands of boys and girls grow up here over the years. Many of them had gone away into the grown-up world imbued with an intangible gift my mother, Aunt Min, had called the "Echo Hill Way." The world, in all this time, had not really become a different or a better place. But the world, as most people knew it, stopped at the Echo Hill cattle guard. Here, everybody was somebody. Everybody had fun. Everybody got to first base once in their lives. Many would, no doubt, be picked off later, but at least they'd had a chance.

Many of the early architects of the "Echo Hill Way" were

now among the missing and missed. My mother had died in 1985. Uncle Floyd Potter, my high school biology teacher and, for many years, our nature-study man, went to Jesus soon after that. Floyd's wife, Aunt Joan, had helped direct the camp for as long as I could remember. Her birthday, August 18, fell on the same date as Min and Tom's anniversary. They had all been very close. Close as the cottonwoods standing by the river.

Slim, too, had passed, as some colloquially refer to dying. Slim had washed dishes, served the "bug juice," and drank warm Jax beer as he listened to the Astros lose a million ball games on his old radio. Death is always colloquial.

Doc and Aunt Hilda Phelps had been the first to go. They'd always been older, I suppose. Doc was Tom's friend from the air force days who helped Tom and Min start the ranch. Hilda, his Australian wife, had taught handicrafts at Echo Hill, and, when I was six years old, had taught me "Waltzing Matilda." For several years I sang the song as "Waltzing with Hilda."

There were many ghosts at Echo Hill, but most of them were friendly. They mixed in quite gracefully with the dust and the campfire smoke and the river and the stars.

Tom was almost all that was left now of the old days. He looked out over the beautiful valley, now quiet except for the horses and the deer. The lights of some of the cabins twinkled merrily. Laughter drifted down from the dining hall, where my sister Marcie was still meeting with some of the counselors. It was hard to believe that within a few days over a hundred kids would be running around the place. It was hard to believe that forty years had gone by and Echo Hill was still the same. Only the names had been changed to protect the innocent.

I opened the gate and walked up the path. Sam, Tom's myopic Jewish shepherd, barked furiously, ran at me, and came within a hair of biting my ass before he recognized me and smiled like a coal-scuttle.

"Sambo!" Tom shouted. "Pick on someone your own size."

"That dog keeps eating like a boar hog," I said as I hugged my father, "we'll have to get him a golf cart."

"Sam's doing fine," said Tom. "Large mammals always put on a little weight in the winter."

Tom would never hear a bad word about Sam. In truth, Sam was a wonderful dog. Tom had gotten him from the pound in the year following my mother's death, and Sam had been a friend indeed. He was a terrific, possibly overzealous watchdog who scared most visitors within an inch of their lives, but he loved children. The only people he hated were teenage boys, people in uniforms, and Mexicans. "What can I say?" Tom had once offered after Sam had chased a Mexican worker onto the roof of the pickup truck. "The dog's a racist."

Tom had put on a little weight himself over the year, adding to an already protuberant abdomen, but he could still whip almost all comers in tennis. Other than an extremely large gut, which he did not recognize he had, he looked very fit and virile.

We talked for a while about the ranch, the staff, the upcoming summer, and, finally, the conversation worked its way around to another matter.

"You got a rather strange message on the machine today from Pat Knox. I still think she did you the greatest favor of your life by keeping you from being elected justice of the peace in Kerrville."

"Yeah," I said. "That could've been ugly. It's a good thing my fellow Kerrverts returned me to the private sector."

"If you'd won that job, what would you have done with it?"

"Pretty much what I'm doing now," I said.

"That's what I was afraid of," said Tom.

I took out a cigar, lopped the butt off, and achieved ignition. I puffed a few easygoing puffs and gazed out over the flat.

"Doesn't the ranch look beautiful?" Tom said.

"Sure does," I said, staring down the quiet, peaceful line of bunkhouses, which appeared to be bracing themselves for an onslaught of shouting, boisterous ranchers. "So what did Pat Knox want?"

"I have no idea," said Tom. "It was strange. She said some things were happening that she didn't understand. She sounded very upset about it. She said she needed to talk to a man of your talents."

"Musical?"

Tom laughed. "Not unless she wants you to perform at somebody's funeral. From her tone, it sounds pretty serious. When she mentioned 'a man of your talents,' I think she must've been referring to some of your forays into crime-solving in New York."

I took a few more thoughtful puffs on the cigar and watched the moon rising over the mountain.

"Or," I said, "she may just want me to drop off her laundry."

★ ★ ★ ★ ★

The next morning with the sun shining brightly on Echo Hill, the nearby mountain from which the camp took its name, I called Pat Knox. It was such a beautiful day that it seemed nothing, with the exception of the cat's not having returned, could be wrong in the world. Of course, Echo Hill was not the world. With a cup of coffee and a cigar under way, I sat at the tiny desk in my trailer and spoke to the secretary at the office of the justice of the peace, precinct one, Kerrville, Texas.

"Oh," said the secretary, "she'll be tickled pink. You're just the person she's been wanting to talk to. She'll be so relieved."

"Relieved?" I said. "Is Kerrville under siege?" I thought of my campaign slogan in my ill-fated race against her boss: "I'll keep us out of war with Fredericksburg." Fredericksburg was a little German town about twenty miles down the road where they still tied their shoes with little Nazis.

"We're not exactly under *siege*, darlin'," she said, "unless you want to count the Yankees, the yuppies, the developers, the retirees—"

"That's what I was hoping to be," I said.

"I think the judge has other ideas," she said.

I held the line and waited. I wondered what was going on. Perhaps Judge Knox had just received word that nine warships had broken through the Confederate blockade. I was pouring another cup of coffee when Her Honor came on the line.

"Can you come into town today?" she said. "I don't want to talk on the phone. There may be spies."

"Spies?" I said. "In Kerrville? Do they wear satellite dishes on their cowboy hats?"

The feisty little judge was not amused. "This is serious," she said. "If what I think is happenin' is really happenin', this little sleepy town is gonna have an ugly awakenin'."

It was a fairly ugly awakening for me, too, I thought. My first day back in Texas, the cat's gone, I'm trying to drink my second cup of coffee, and I'm already being sucked into some kind of foreign intrigue. Of all the happy campers who'd soon be at the ranch, I was definitely not one. With the cat gone, there wasn't even anyone around to talk to. When you have to talk to a cat that isn't there, you might as well be talking to yourself.

I poured a third cup of coffee, lit a second cigar, and wandered over to see my kid sister next door. Marcie, who, along with Tom, directed the camp, lived in a big white trailer that looked as if it had belonged in its first life to Jim Rockford. Marcie was very busy getting the camp ready to open and she was also having some trouble getting her eyes open because she'd stayed up so late meeting with the staff. She did not display a great deal of concern about the cat being missing.

"I'm sure your cat will come back," she said.

"I don't know," I said. "This has never happened before."

"It may never happen again, either," she said. "Especially if Sambo gets hold of the cat."

I paced up and down Marcie's trailer as she was getting dressed, forgetting how much my cigar smoke always irritated her when she first woke up. Of course, almost everything irritated Marcie when she first woke up. She, as siblings often will, believed that it was I who was the grumpy one and that she herself had a constantly cheery, pleasant disposition. Both of us frequently confronted Tom with the well-considered opinion that he was grumpier than either of us. Tom would either laugh it off or sullenly deny it, depending on how grumpy he was feeling at the time. Whenever he laughed it off, it usually made me and Marcie pretty grumpy.

"I mourn the fact," I said, "that young people today don't drink coffee and that they don't have more compassion for cats."

"I mourn the fact," said Marcie, "that I've got exactly one day to get this camp open and somebody's marching up and down my trailer smoking a cigar when I'm trying to get dressed."

"I mourn the fact," I said, "that more effort hasn't been made on the part of the directors to more fully integrate me into the camp program."

"I mourn the fact," said Marcie, "that you won't get your ass out of my trailer."

I walked up to the lodge just as Tom was filling the hummingbird feeders. The lodge was set in an area surrounded by a white wooden fence to keep the horses out, which it rarely did. Eighty-seven trees grew inside the fence, according to Tom. One of them, very close to the lodge, was dead. That was the one the hummingbirds always established as their home base when they returned to the Hill Country from South America or wherever the hell hummingbirds come from. They arrived punctually on March 15 and stayed until about the end of August. It was a good thing they weren't housepests.

More than thirty years ago, my mother had started feeding the hummingbirds, dissolving sugar in red-dyed water and hanging the glass feeders on the eaves of the porch. The job had now devolved to Tom and myself. There were more than fifty hummingbirds around now, and during happy hour things could get pretty busy. I thought of Tom as my assistant hummingbird feeder. He thought of me as his assistant hummingbird feeder. Somehow, we managed.

Tom was hanging the last feeder on a nail and Ben Stroud was walking behind him trying to make up a list of things to get in town.

"Why are you following me?" Tom said to Ben.

Ben, aware that this was pretty much of a rhetorical question, did not give an answer. Instead, in the manner of a Talmudic scholar, he asked another question.

"Should I get the paper for you in town?" he asked. "I'm getting the laundry and the softballs and the donuts."

"I could get Tom's paper," I said to Ben. "I'm going into Kerrville for lunch."

"No, I'll get it," said Ben. "I've got a whole list of shit to do."

Tom walked over to the redwood furniture, which was

older than most of the counselors, and sat down in his favorite chair. Ben wandered over to check a thing or two on his
town list.

"Why are you following me?" Tom said to Ben.

Tom and Ben and I sat and talked for a while, then they
both had things to do. I wandered around the ranch like a
stray horse for about an hour, talked to a few of the old counselors who were getting their activities set up, and ran into
Marcie down at the picnic area. We'd both gotten over our little sibling snit from earlier that morning.

"Care to join me for lunch at the Del Norte?" I asked.

"I've got to stay here," she said. "Camp's starting tomorrow, one of the cooks hasn't shown up yet, and Tom snapped
his wig this morning when he couldn't find a typewriter rib-
bon. Who are you having lunch with?"

"The Honorable Pat Knox," I said.

"Pat Knox? Isn't she the one who beat you like a drum in
the election?"

"I'm not bitter," I said.

I saddled up Dusty, my mother's old wood-paneled Chrysler
convertible, waved at my cousin Bucky, who was rounding up
horses on the East Flat, and headed into Kerrville. I was thinking I could use a little liquor drink to cut the phlegm. I was also
thinking how being here at camp would, of necessity, cut into
my cocktail hour. My normal habits and lifestyle in New York
were not especially healthy for green plants or children. Not
that I was a role model particularly. I just felt that if kids were
going to screw up their lives, they ought to figure out how to
do it themselves.

Dusty was a talking car. My mother had always said it was

a good car for lonely people. I hadn't been back long enough to know whether or not I was lonely yet, but I was interested in hearing what Dusty had to say. As I drove down the gravel county road to the highway, Dusty demonstrated just how perceptive she was.

"Your washer fluid is low," she said.

"I want to talk to you," said Pat Knox in deeply conspiratorial tones, "about four little old ladies." We were sitting at a corner table in the Del Norte Restaurant, a place I'd often referred to as the best restaurant in the world. At least it was the best restaurant in Kerrville.

"Four little old ladies?" I said. "Do they want me to join a quilting bee?"

"No," said the little judge. "They're dead."

"Eighty-six that quilting bee."

"If you're just gonna make fun of me, I might as well be talking to the sheriff. That's what she did, too."

Not for the first time did I think what a strange town was Kerrville, Texas. For decades it had enjoyed a redneck macho milieu, overpopulated with pickup trucks sporting loaded gun racks in their rear windows. Now, suddenly, Kerrville had a lady sheriff and a lady justice of the peace. What was the world coming to?

The judge summoned up all the dignity and controlled

anger within her four foot eleven and one-half inch frame, which was fairly considerable when she stared at you across the table. I sipped my coffee and hoped the waitress would bring me my chicken fried steak before Pat Knox reached into her leather briefcase and pulled out a pearl-handled Beretta.

"When I first met you during the campaign," she said, "I didn't like you."

"Quite understandable," I said. "I have a certain superficial charm that holds up for about three minutes when I meet people. After that, it's usually downhill."

"I must've stayed around for five minutes," she said, as she reached into her leather briefcase. I readied myself.

As fate would have it, she only extracted a sheaf of papers, but in her eyes I could still see the Beretta.

"It was later in the campaign, Richard," she said, using my Christian name, "that I met you one day in the bank, and thought I saw that you were really a gentleman."

"We all make mistakes," I said.

"I don't think I made one," she said.

I had become so accustomed to dealing with NYPD types that I almost didn't realize that this little woman was complimenting me and asking for my help. I didn't really see how I could help and I wasn't even sure what the problem was, but I felt a little ashamed about being a smart-ass. Maybe all law enforcement people brought it out in me.

The waitress came with our orders just as Pat was showing me a map of the Texas Hill Country with four little X's scattered around a fairly wide area.

"Each X indicates an isolated location in which one of these old ladies—all of them were widows—lived. And died."

I studied the map politely as I cut into my chicken fried steak.

"The sheriff has listed the deaths as accidental, natural, or suicide. She feels that four deaths in five months does not establish any kind of pattern and I can't say I really disagree with her about that. Anyway, I don't have the power to call for a formal investigation."

I took a bite of chicken fried steak. It's an over-ordered dish in Texas and most of the time it's nothing you'd want to write home about even if you had a home. I was wondering what Pat was getting at. Did she want me to share her work load? That would've taken a lot of nerve after vanquishing me in the election.

"The first lady drowned in the bathtub near Bandera—"

"Household accident number 437," I said.

"The second burned to death in her home near Pipe Creek."

"Did she run back in trying to fetch her pipe?"

Pat Knox looked at me with disappointment in her eyes. The look quickly changed to a flat, hard, tail-gunner's expression.

"The third death occurred near Mountain Home. The victim was shot with a gun. The weapon was found near the body."

"That was the suicide?"

"You New Yorkers sure don't miss a beat."

"Hold the weddin'," I said. "I come from Texas."

"You could've fooled me."

"And it's no disgrace to come from Texas," I said. "It's just a disgrace to have to come back here."

Her Honor laughed briefly. I assured her I was kidding. She continued reading her book of the dead and I continued eating my chicken fried steak which I hoped was dead.

"The fourth death occurred just outside of town on the road to Ingram. The woman required an oxygen supply and apparently the bottle had come disconnected. That's it."

"That's it?"

"Now three of the deaths didn't even occur in this county, so they're not really my jurisdiction—"

"Or mine."

"That's correct. But I've talked to other J.P.'s, to members of the families. I've conducted my own private investigation— I always do. Crime scenes, blood splatters, photos. I've kept records on all of this."

I was only half listening now. I was thinking how a handful of deaths of elderly people wouldn't amount to a hill of beans in crazy old New York. It wouldn't even make good table conversation. I wondered again why the judge had called me. Did she want to show me how hard the job was and how overworked she was? Was she trying to rub it in that I'd lost the election?

"Okay, Pat, so what's all this mean? Put it on a bumper sticker for me."

"I know they were murdered."

Great, I thought. The whole thing is coming down like some gothic novel. Pat Knox is Joan of Arc. Pat Knox is Cassandra warning the warriors of Troy. Pat Knox is Martha Mitchell reporting that Secret Service agents had kidnapped her and shot her in the butt with a hypodermic needle. Who listens to these people? No one. Not until a little B&E job at

Watergate brings down a presidency. Not until the Trojan Horse is taken into the gates of the city. Not until we all can hear the voices that once were only in Joan's head.

"I believe you," I said.

The judge sighed deeply. "But there's more," she said. "When I was a child I witnessed sexual molestation occurring for a period of several years within the family next door. I'm almost psychic about any aura of sexual violence in the air."

I sipped my coffee and waited.

"I know this sounds crazy," she said. "But I also believe they were raped."

"Pat," I said, "the sheriff is very well-liked around here and by all accounts very efficient. In fact, as you know, she just solved a triple murder case recently. Maybe she *is* investigating and just chooses not to tell you." I could understand why the sheriff might not take the judge to her bosom, so to speak.

"I hope to hell you're right," she said, " 'cause I'm damn near worried sick about this."

"Remember what Mark Twain said: 'I've had many troubles in my life, but most of them never happened.' "

The judge did not look convinced. She picked up her briefcase and stood up, indicating that our little luncheon was over.

"Tell that to Nigger Jim," she said.

8

★ ★ ★ ★ ★

The following night, ten little girls stood outside the green trailer in the moonlight. It was pushing Cinderella time. They were all in their pajamas and many of them had brought cameras. They were hoping to get a picture of Dilly. He was there, too. Dilly was my pet armadillo.

There are those who say armadillos do not make good animal companions, but they have obviously never known the joys of tickling one behind its ears or hearing it knocking on their trailer door in the early hours of the morning for a midnight snack of milk, bacon grease, and cat food. There was a note of sadness in my heart as I brought the cat food out to Dilly amidst the throng of giggling, awestruck members of the Bluebonnets. I had a lot of cat food, I reflected, for a man without a cat.

The Bluebonnets and Dilly, however, were oblivious to my own personal sorrows. Dilly was enjoying himself immensely, and quite frequently, rising to the occasion on his two hind claws. Whenever this happened, the flash of paparazzi cameras fairly lasered the darkness of the surrounding cedar trees.

There was something rather poignant, almost spiritual, about the little scene. For armadillos, as practically every Texan knows, are the very shyest of creatures, who, ironically, have been fated to co-inhabit a state populated with the very loudest, brashest of human beings. Nevertheless, they've been here since the time of the dinosaurs, and they're not about to let a silly race of people 86 them out this late in the game.

For those who are not intimately familiar with the armadillo, it is a small, armored creature about the size of . . . well, a cat. Its shell, as John D. MacDonald once observed, is often made into baskets and sold by the roadside. MacDonald also expressed a wish that somewhere in the universe there existed a planet inhabited by sentient armadillos who carved out humans and sold them as baskets by the roadside.

"Can armadillos hurt you?" asked Marisa.

"No," I said. "Only people can."

"Is Dilly going to have a baby?" asked Michelle.

"No, Dilly is a boy. And armadillos never have just one baby; they always have a litter of four. And the four are always either all boys or all girls." I was quite an armadillologist.

"Can we pat Dilly?" asked Alene.

"Of course," I said. "But do it gently or you'll scare him. Armadillos almost never get this close to people. Dilly is a very special armadillo."

The girls crowded around Dilly and he seemed to luxuriate in all the attention. Some of them stroked his armored shell. Some tickled him behind the ears. He even posed for pictures with the girls like a little primeval spirit come to save the world from itself. For some only slightly sick reason, I thought of Christ in the manger.

"Of course," I said, "armadillos have been known to carry leprosy."

The two counselors stiffened and recoiled a bit, but the Bluebonnets remained in their attentive circle around Dilly.

"What's leprosy?" asked Jessica.

"Disease where your nose falls off," I said.

The girls stopped petting Dilly and looked at me with that serious, half-believing expression children sometimes acquire when they suspect the adult they're listening to may be insane. I shrugged.

"Don't worry," I said. "They don't pass it along to people. Only to other armadillos. Besides, Dilly's already been up to the infirmary and the nurse gave him a health check."

As if to demonstrate his general fitness, Dilly jumped about two feet in the air, then bolted inside the trailer with about six little girls almost literally on his tail. Like a young rhinoceros, he slammed into everything in sight, knocking over the forlorn bowls of cat food and water, my guitar, and a small lamp. At incredible land speeds he scooted across the floor, back and forth, with the screaming Bluebonnets alternately running after him and then away from him. Eventually, he bolted out the door and into the night, and I began attempting to shoehorn personnel out of the trailer and back to their bunk.

"What's this?" asked Briana, holding up a piece of paper.

I glanced at the page. It was a sketch of Kerr, Bandera, and several neighboring counties. Four black X's appeared at various loci on the paper.

"Where'd you get this, Bri?"

★   ★   ★   **44**   ★   ★   ★

"I found it on the floor," she said.

I looked at the page again. This time, with the little girls standing around me under the moonlight, an almost palpable evil seemed to emanate from it.

"Is it a treasure map?" Bri shouted.

"No," I said. "It's Dilly's health chart."

At roughly 2:09 in the morning, in the middle of a rather gnarly nightmare about little girls transforming instantaneously into little old ladies, I woke up suddenly to hear a thump on the nonfunctioning air conditioner outside my window. Moments later, the cat jumped through the open window and, either deliberately or accidentally, landed on my testicles.

Chapter

9

★ ★ ★ ★ ★

I woke up the next morning to the ringing of the old bell by the office and the sounds of radio station ECHO echoing off the hills. The disc jockey, Alex Hoffman, sometimes referred to as Phallax Hoseman, ran the station out of the media room. His first selection, unfortunately, was "The Purple People Eater." ECHO was staffed and run by the ranchers, but it still reflected Phallax's rather eclectic influence, ranging from "Wipe-Out" to early Bob Dylan, to "Happy Birthday from the Army," to "Schwinn 24" by a little-known Texas group called "King Arthur and the Carrots." ECHO, at Hoseman's behest, also played Harry Chapin's "Cat's in the Cradle" at least two hundred times a day.

The cat was sleeping beside me on the bed and, except for a rather irritated look in her eye, showed no signs of joining me to face the day. It was quite evident, however, from the way she was twitching her left ear, that she did not like the song "Purple People Eater."

"I'll be sure to mention it to Phallax," I told her, as I put on my boots, opened the creaky door of the green trailer, and stared at the large porthole painting of a cross section of a watermelon. The painting had been done many years ago by a talented, somewhat eccentric counselor named Jules LeMelle who'd insisted that his only free time to do the work was at 6:00 A.M. So he'd painted the door and one inner wall of the trailer in a watermelon motif over a period of about a week while I tried to sleep with some weird guy drawing psychedelic watermelon designs inside my trailer.

LeMelle had gotten the idea from a story I'd told him about a Kappa Alpha fraternity float I'd once seen in a parade at the University of Texas. The float, as I remembered it, had been a huge construction of a watermelon with live little black children dancing around on it, ostensibly representing the seeds. It'd happened so long ago that, if I hadn't known better, I'd have thought I'd dreamed it. But it had happened, I had mentioned it to Jules LeMelle, and he'd painted psychedelic watermelons all over the inner wall and door of my trailer. The natural green color of the outside of the trailer served as a perfect giant watermelon rind for the pink porthole painting when the door was closed.

As I walked up the little road to the dining hall to get some of Rosie's coffee, a dim memory of the Kappa Alpha float passed by in my mind again. Racism was easier to spot in those days. So was Jules LeMelle, for that matter. I wondered very briefly what ever had happened to him. I also wondered very briefly what ever had happened to all the rest of us.

I walked into the dining hall with the old ranch brands still on the rafters where Aunt Hilda had painted them forty years ago. The tables and chairs all looked bright and cheerful now that the kids were back. They'd been sitting alone all winter. The giant Mexican chess sets stood, with tall kings and queens, bishops, rooks, knights, pawns all in a row, each waiting for little hands. Darkened old black-and-white photos on the walls. A row of little girls standing together in front of their bunkhouse in 1953. I recognized Bunny Slipakoff, my first girlfriend, standing shyly on the right-hand side. I thought it was Bunny.

I went over to the giant lumberjack coffee urn. On the wall beside it hung the large Navajo sand painting Doc and Aunt Hilda had brought back from their stay on the reservation. The painting had hung there as long as I could remember. Now Doc and Aunt Hilda were gone and the sand painting was still there. I drew a cup of coffee and sat down alone at one of the long tables. I sipped the coffee and let my eyes gently wash across the sand painting. It was replete with suns and stars and dancers and animals and rainbows. I sipped some more coffee and noticed that the colors were still as bright as I remembered them. Forty years was a long time to a rainbow.

I looked over the counter into the kitchen and saw Elese sitting at the table sculpting orthodox rabbi heads or something out of lettuce. Rosie, the Hawaiian cook, came out of the kitchen into the dining hall and offered me one of her homemade sweet rolls.

"That's the best offer I've had today," I said.

"I can't believe that," said Rosie. She was a great cook, played the ukulele, and gave an excellent haircut.

"What's for dinner tonight?"

"Hamburgers," she said. "Down at the picnic area."

"Sambo usually eats about twelve of them," I said.

"He does like my cookin'," said Rosie. "I don't think it's nice that some of the counselors call him 'Cujo.' "

Rosie went back to the kitchen and I wandered over to the Crafts Corral, where Eric Roth, with about ten kids surrounding him, was checking out the kiln. Ceramic leaf ashtrays were always a happening thing at Echo Hill. Almost no one on the planet smoked anymore but still we turned out hundreds of ceramic leaf ashtrays. I wasn't sure what today's beleaguered parents could use them for. Maybe paperweights for their divorce papers.

At a far table, engulfed by a mob of eager ranchers, stood Aunt Anita. Today, Aunt Anita appeared to be teaching the kids how to make the ever-popular "monkey's fist," but, in truth, there was almost nothing Aunt Anita couldn't construct out of string. Maybe, I thought, I should put her in touch with Pat Knox.

I stood at the window outside the Crafts Corral and noticed that Eric had a new assistant. She was bending over the kiln and from where I was standing, behind her, she looked like she was going to be a big boost to a lot more than just the handicrafts program. She seemed to have been delicately formed on some celestial potter's wheel.

"Pam's from Oklahoma," Eric said, following my gaze.

"I'm Richard Kinky 'Big Dick' Friedman," I said by way of introduction. "And I never met a Pam I didn't like."

Pam had short blond hair and green, partly cloudy eyes that seemed to cut into me like dust blowing across the barren landscape of my soul.

"What's the 'Big Dick' stand for?" she said.

The little repartee was interrupted by Eddie Wolff, a huge,

gentle counselor and wrangler, shouting from the office like a giant, slightly agitated teddy bear you knew you'd better listen to. There was a long-distance phone call for me, apparently. Of course, being so far from the city, every call that came into the ranch was long distance.

I went over to the office, picked up the blower, and heard Pat Knox's secretary, Paula, tell me to hold on for the judge. I hadn't thought about the judge for about nine hours and I was feeling pretty good about it.

"Have you gone over the material I gave you?" Pat asked.

"I've started," I lied. "Been kind of busy here lately unpacking my Frisbee. Doing squat thrusts in the parking lot."

"Get crackin'," she said. "There's gonna be a full moon out tonight. Lots of strange critters'll be stirrin'."

I walked out of the office, past two new counselors I didn't recognize who were taking down the big WELCOME RANCHERS sign on the bulletin board. Walking along the dusty road to the green trailer I heard a New York angel whisper in my ear. "Don't get involved," it said.

I opened the door to the trailer and saw that the cat was in precisely the same position she was lying in when I left. As I walked across the floor to the little desk she opened her eyes.

"Pat Knox is as crazy as a betsy-bug," I said.

The cat looked at me, yawned, then closed her eyes.

"I know what you mean," I said.

It was almost Gary Cooper time and I was sitting out behind the trailer in the hot sun alternately watching the river flow and forking through the folder Pat Knox had given me. It wasn't clear that I was getting anywhere but at least I was working on my tan. All I was wearing were my Jesus boots, the same bathing suit I'd owned for twenty-five years, and an increasingly surly expression.

"I don't understand the purpose of the exercise," I said to the cat, who sat on the large wooden spool that served as a table.

The cat said nothing. She didn't understand the exercise either. She didn't even understand why we'd come to Texas.

"If I keep reading these morbid, stultifyingly dull coroner's reports," I said, "I'm going to jump in the river and drown."

The cat stared at me, then gazed out at the river. Her placid, agreeable expression seemed to indicate that she thought it might not be such a bad idea.

"We don't really consider it a river," I said. "Around here

folks call it a crick. Big Foot Wallace Crick, to be precise. Named after Big Foot Wallace, a famous frontier scout who lived with the Indians."

The cat took on a very bored countenance. The only remote interest she had in Native Americans was that they occasionally wore feathers.

Reluctantly, I returned to Pat Knox's papers. They didn't exactly make for riveting summer reading. As she'd already told me, three of the four deaths had occurred outside her bailiwick, and there was no firsthand information here relating to them. What there was were sketchy, hearsay little short stories that you could've read to a bunch of kids if you wanted to bore them to sleep. Worse, from my point of view, there was not even the whiff of a nuance of foul play in any of the three. The closest to it was the first case, the lady who'd drowned in her bathtub in Bandera. A neighbor of the deceased told Pat's mother, Dot, that she could've sworn the woman never took a bath.

The death by fire in Pipe Creek was nothing but smoke and mirrors, and every time I looked into one of the mirrors I saw Pat Knox staring back at me like the Mad Lady of Chaillot.

"She *is* crazy as a betsy-bug," I said to the cat. The cat lay like a waxen figure on the tabletop.

"*One* of us is crazy as a betsy-bug," I said.

The cat did not respond.

The description of the third death, near Mountain Home, in which a gun was found near the body, at least demonstrated a colorful command of the vernacular on the part of that town's octogenarian justice of the peace, John Hill. "The bullet," Hill reportedly had said, "didn't have no reverse on it.

It went in the back of her head like it had eyes, but when it went out, I'll be damned if it didn't have a nose."

The fourth death, the one that had taken place in Judge Knox's precinct, was the most recent, having occurred just two weeks earlier. The good judge had not only composed a mordant document that was as interminable as a Homeric lyrical poem; it might as well have been Greek. Her notes looked like they'd been written by a mariner crab.

The cat got up, stood on the paper, and gazed down with a quite perplexed expression.

"Jesus," I said. "Somebody gave me the wrong Torah portion."

The cat said nothing. She was of an extremely secular bent and could not be drawn easily into conversations of a religious nature. This was, quite possibly, to her credit. I've known a lot of cats in my life who've gotten all worked up on the subject. Of course, when you have nine lives, it doesn't matter if you're dead wrong eight times.

The lady who'd died recently, the fourth in the supposed string that stretched between Pat Knox's ears like the lonely string of colored lights they always hung across the road in Medina at Christmastime, was seventy-five years old and had required a special oxygen supply. Maybe the bottle had become disconnected accidentally, or maybe someone had deliberately . . .

"Goddamnit," I said. "Move your foot!"

The cat glared at me, then, rather grudgingly, moved off the paper. Cats have an uncanny ability to find precisely that particular patch of paper which you're trying to read. They find it and they proceed to stand, sit, or lie down on only that portion which is germane. Indeed, if editors, lawyers, and amateur private detectives were more patient, they could avoid reading reams of irrelevant material. They could just light up cigars, sit back, and let cats settle on the document in question.

In this case, it wouldn't have worked. There was nothing in the judge's papers that suggested any pattern, any foul play, or, I might add, any particular grasp on reality. The part the cat had obscured merely noted that the victim, Prudence South, had, as a hobby, made little hats for cats. The fact that the cat had chosen this information to obfuscate might be cosmic, or might've had a certain significance to the cat, but it meant nothing to me. Except that I was damn sure going to let Pat Knox attack her own windmills.

I stacked the papers neatly and placed an eighty-million-year-old fossil on top of them as a paperweight.

"Wish I was that well preserved," I said.

The cat did not reply. Tact was not her long suit, but she knew better than to poke fun at the middle-aged.

I leaned back and lit a cigar and for a while the two of us sat peacefully behind the green trailer in the sunshine of that little valley and watched the river flow. It flowed under a little red wooden bridge, past sycamore and cypress trees, past beautiful banks of natural rock, over the dam that Earl Buckelew had built over fifty years ago, and on down to Big Foot Falls, also of course, named after Big Foot Wallace.

As I sat there, a great sense of peace and calm invaded my somewhat weatherbeaten spirit. The travails of New York City, the urgent scrawlings of Judge Knox, my own private loneliness of heart, began to float away on the currents of the little sunlit stream. It seemed almost to be murmuring to me, and I thought of the old camp song my mother had always liked: "Peace I ask of thee, O river, / Peace, peace, peace."

The next thing I knew the bell was ringing and the quiet of siesta was over. What appeared to be at least three bunkhouses of ranchers began boisterously descending upon the green trailer and the little stream beyond for their shallow-water swimming tests. The cat, a black and white cartoon character, shot off the table and into the bowels of the trailer like a missile seeking peace. But peace, as so many children of the world have learned, is harder to find than tits on a mule.

Chapter

★ ★ ★ ★ ★

The first few days of camp went by like a scorpion skittering across a bunkhouse floor. The troubled outside world disappeared and was replaced, for all practical purposes, by cookouts, water fights, horseback riding, softball games, and isolated spates of homesickness that soon gave way to unbridled fun. The gray, desperate adult world all but vanished in the world of sunshine and childhood at Echo Hill.

As for me, the specter of murder and mayhem had been pushed to a dark corner table of my mind and the cruelty and suffering that grown-ups routinely inflicted upon other grown-ups was simply not on the menu. The most serious altercation I'd allowed myself to become involved in was one night when I entered the Bronco Busters bunkhouse and broke up a pillow fight. My universe was demarcated by a circle of hills; the only things that mattered were the ones that occurred within that little green valley.

"It's so peaceful," I said to Pam as I stood by the window of the Crafts Corral. "Makes you want to just resign from the human race. Maybe I'll retire."

"What is it you'd retire from?" she said.

"That's a good question. I see you're ignorant of my talents."

"Totally," said Pam, but she smiled a quick, mischievous smile to mollify what she imagined to be my wounded ego. She didn't realize that I'd left it on a curb in New York many years ago.

"Had a country band once. In the early seventies. Kinky Friedman and the Texas Jewboys. We toured the country and irritated a lot of Americans. Now I sing mostly at campfires, whorehouses, the occasional bar mitzvah."

"The only thing I remember about the seventies," said Pam, "was getting my first tricycle for Christmas." She turned her back to me for a moment and bent down to select some paint from a cabinet. I almost swallowed my cigar.

"It stands to reason you never heard of me," I said. "You were jumping rope in the schoolyard when I was ordering room service. Also, Oklahoma isn't the bar mitzvah capital of the world."

"Not like Texas?"

"There's a lot of Jews in Texas, actually. I'm just the oldest living one who doesn't own any real estate. But I'm glad you never heard of me. I've had my share of groupies."

"I don't think you'll have to worry," she said.

I had her right where I wanted her, I thought, as I wandered away in the direction of the Nature Shack. She probably didn't realize that, after a few more weeks of isolation from the outside, Echo Hill took on almost the sexual ambience of a bar at closing time. All I had to do was play my cards right. I didn't know of anyone who'd really done that yet, but there was always a first time. In life, they don't always remember to cut the deck.

That night I stood in the shadows of the campfire and watched the children watching the fire. Their eyes reflected a bright hope you didn't see much on the streets of the city. Any city. I was about to play a song for the kids and Marcie was introducing me. The atmosphere backstage was quite relaxed, more so even than when I drank a very large amount of Jack Daniel's at the Lone Star Café in New York and had to be rolled onstage on a gurney.

Except for the few kids who always shine their flashlights in your face, it was a pretty good crowd. Some familiar faces, some new ones. Not your glitzy New York–L.A.-type audience. Just a large, cheerful group of young kids sitting on blankets in their bunkhouse groups, far away from home but close to the campfire. The ceiling was glittering with stars and the crickets provided a nice little rhythm section. It was a good room to work.

I sang a song that was always quite popular at camp. I'd written it when I was just eleven years old, standing backstage rehearsing for my bar mitzmas with my little yamaha on my head. The lyrics went as follows:

> *Ol' Ben Lucas*
> *Had a lot of mucus*
> *Comin' right out of his nose.*
> *He'd pick and pick*

*'Til it made you sick
But back again it grows.*

*When it's cotton-pickin' time in Texas
Boys, it's booger-pickin' time for Ben.
He'd raise that finger, mean and hostile,
Stick it in that waiting nostril
Here he comes with a green one once again.*

Everybody sang the "Ol' Ben Lucas" chorus several more times, then I ankled it out of there with Marcie shouting, "Let's give Kinky a big 1-2-3 HOW!!!" The ranchers all joined in on the 1-2-3 HOW part, which was the equivalent of applause in the city, and they shouted it as loudly and as sharply as they could, an act that generated countless echoes off the surrounding hills.

I wasn't as pumped up as James Brown after a show, but it did feel good hearing the echoes as I packed up my guitar and slipped off into the dark, beautiful, anonymous night. Every performer, no matter how great, is a ham at heart. Whether you're playing Carnegie Hall or a campfire for kids, it's still another show in your hip pocket.

Part of my job at camp, along with the overwhelming responsibility of being hummingbird man and occasionally dropping off laundry in town, was security. Not that anyone expected six Islamic fundamentalists in a blue sedan to drive up to the flagpole. I was just supposed to walk around, turn on some of the lights at night, and, as Tom says, "maintain a presence." It wasn't very difficult. I'd been doing it most of my life.

The ranch was eerily silent with the kids all out at the

campfire. The cat was sitting on top of the trailer watching the horses grazing on the latest project by the Echo Hill Garden Club. The Echo Hill Garden Club didn't usually have a lot of luck. If the horses didn't eat their latest project, the deer invariably would. Not only did we not get the opportunity to reap what we sowed, we rarely got a chance to even see it.

I'd put my guitar up and was just lighting a cigar and pouring a little shot when the phone rang.

"Start talkin'," I said.

"This is Pat." I didn't have to ask, Pat who? I was currently a one-Pat man.

"Yes, Pat," I said patiently.

"There's been another one."

I took a couple of paternalistic puffs on the cigar.

"Pat, there's always going to be another one. These are little old ladies. Little old ladies are mortal. When their time comes they fall through the trapdoor just like everybody else, no matter how hard they've crammed for the final exam."

With the hand that wasn't holding the blower, I lifted the shot of Jack Daniel's from my faithful old bullhorn and discharged it into my mouth. The little judge was really starting to get up my sleeve. I poured another small shot.

"She was murdered," said Pat stubbornly.

"How do you know that?" I fairly shouted. "Did she come back and appear to you in a séance and tell you that?"

"She couldn't have done that," said the judge. "Her lips were sewn shut."

★ ★ ★ ★ ★

As I entered the old courthouse the next morning I thought of the only time I'd ever seen anybody's lips sewn shut. It'd been many years ago and the lips had belonged to the shrunken head in the Bandera museum. The sight hadn't been pleasant on a head the size of a tennis ball, and I could only too well imagine the nightmare vision of an actual-size human face mutilated in the same macabre fashion. It was enough to put you right off your huevos rancheros.

The old courthouse hadn't really come to life yet, if it ever did. The old lady who'd been spliced the night before wouldn't be coming to life again either, unless it was to haunt my dreams someday when I was tucked away in the Shalom Retirement Village.

The halls seemed empty as my heart. I walked past some old wooden doors that looked like they'd been closed for a hundred years, some pebbled glass, and about seven spittoons. Before I knew it I was sitting in a big office in front of a big desk behind which sat a big woman. Everything was big in Texas, I thought. Even the small towns.

"The old lady who died last night," I said. "The one with her lips sewn shut. That one definitely goes down as murder, right?"

"Of *course* it was murder," said Sheriff Frances Kaiser, looking fairly murderous herself. "Can you think of anything else you could call it?"

"There's always the possibility," I said, "that she might've had a nearsighted tailor?"

I chuckled a brief, good-natured chuckle. A large vein throbbed in the sheriff's neck.

"What in the dickens would lead you to believe it *wasn't* murder?" she said. "Poor old thing was strangled and her lips sewn shut. Doesn't that sound like murder to you? Maybe you've been in New York too long."

"This kind of wanton violence never happens in New York," I said. "We're all good, God-fearin' little church workers up there. Mind if I smoke?"

The sheriff gave an expansive, almost papal, wave as if she were shooing away an extremely large gnat. I fished around for a cigar in the many pockets of my beaded Indian vest. This created an awkward moment and, by the time I found the cigar and started setting fire to it, I could see that the sheriff was fresh out of charm.

Sheriff Frances Kaiser was no one to putz around with. She was a big, tall, no-nonsense type who'd grown up on a ranch near Medina. As a kid, she'd done chores around the ranch and driven the tractor. Now, in her first term in office, she was one hell of a mean-looking sheriff. I could tell she was past wondering what I was doing in her office. Through the blue cigar smoke I heard her speaking to me.

"We've heard tales of your exploits in New York. Any truth to them?"

"There's a little. You know how those New Yorkers like to brag. I was just wondering whether you had any leads in this latest case."

"Are you offerin' us your expert help?"

"Hell, no. I figure you'd probably have things just about wrapped up by now."

"And you'd be right," said the sheriff, her eyes straying to a gun on her desk. "We've already apprehended a prime suspect and the D.A.'s convening the grand jury to get the indictment."

"Jesus. I thought the mills of justice were supposed to grind slowly but exceedingly fine."

"Those're the mills of the Lord," she corrected. "The mills of justice grind just about as fast as I tell 'em to. Don't you know about the mills of the Lord? It's in the Bible. Your people wrote it."

"Sure, we wrote it. But we didn't like it all that much. We loved the movie."

The room was rapidly beginning to fill up with cigar smoke and unpleasant vibes. It was difficult to pry any information from Sheriff Kaiser without mentioning Pat Knox and, from what I'd already gleaned, mentioning Pat Knox to the sheriff could be lethal. It would totally disseminate what rancid crust of credibility I'd managed to attain. Apparently, my "exploits in New York" had impressed Kaiser about as much as my cowboy hat impressed Sergeant Mort Cooperman in the city.

Well, you can't please 'em all. The only one who seemed to believe in my talents was Pat Knox, and she barely came up to Sheriff Kaiser's kneecap.

"Who's the suspect?" I said.

"I can't tell you that," she snapped.

"Is there anything you *can* tell me besides get the hell out of your office?"

Sheriff Kaiser looked at me stonily. I was glad I wasn't being hauled up here for stealing my neighbor's goat. I waited.

"We're really very busy," said the sheriff, as she studied her fingernails. She performed this gesture, I noticed, not with her palm outward as a woman might, but palm inward with fingers curled toward her, as somebody who drove a tractor might.

"I guess I'll wait till another time," I said, "to ask you to quash my parking tickets."

"Cut the bullshit," she said. "I'm late for my Rotary luncheon." She stood up. She looked bigger than God, even if you happened to be an agnostic.

"Just tell me. Do you think this murder could be related to the other deaths?"

"What other deaths?" said Kaiser irritably.

"You know, Sheriff. The little old ladies."

"Goddamnit, you been talkin' to Pat Knox," said the sheriff, moving toward me like an angry tractor. "Sure you have! That's how you knew about that old lady's lips sewn shut. What else did our wonderfully imaginative justice of the peace tell you?"

"Well, she just thinks there might be some possible connec-tion—"

"There ain't no connection," shouted the sheriff. "Her brain ain't even connected! Her job is to identify the victim— not to run her own investigation! This is a retirement community. There's lots of elderly people here and sooner or later they die. We got a prime suspect right over there in the jail. But we ain't accusin' him of killin' every old person that kicks the bucket. Now you stay the hell out of this! And stop listenin' to Pat Knox!"

Like a kid following behind a fast-moving plow I followed Sheriff Kaiser out of the office.

"I always suspected she was crazy as a betsy-bug," I said.

13

★ ★ ★ ★ ★

Dark thoughts were line dancing through my mind as I hustled my butt over to the Butt-Holdsworth Memorial Library.
Somebody was right and somebody was wrong, and damned
if I needed to get myself square in the middle of an Old West
shoot-out between the female sheriff and the female justice of
the peace. I longed for the days when men were men and
chickens were highly agitato.

My library card had expired back when Christ was a cowboy but I didn't intend to check out any books. All I needed
was information about some people who'd checked out. If
this had been New York I'd just call McGovern and have him
run down the obits for me. Here I'd have to look them up myself. It was tough being your own legman.

I backed the little convertible out of the courthouse parking
lot and promptly became tied up in traffic. For a small town,
Kerrville was coming on strong in the gridlock department.
Of course, in New York I wouldn't have been driving. I'd have
been sitting peacefully behind some guy in a turban who was

honking his horn, shooting the finger, and screaming Sri Lankan death threats. Here, I was waiting for an ancient Studebaker that appeared to have only been driven to church and bingo games to turn left, right, or back into me. At the wheel was a little old lady who barely reached the dash.

A little old lady.

Why was I going to the Butt-Holdsworth Memorial Library to read obits? I was supposed to be on sabbatical, leaving big-city crime and strife behind me in the big city where it belonged. I should listen to the sheriff, whether or not I respected authority figures as large as tractors. They had a little murder. They caught the suspect. The grand jury was going to indict him. The mills of the Lord would keep grinding just like my teeth. People lived and when they got o-l-d they died. Pat Knox had obviously been taking Slim lessons. Slim, in his last few years when he lived alone on the ranch in the wintertime, claimed he was seeing children in trees.

There were no children in trees. And, most likely, there was no succession of little old ladies upon whom some unknown fiend was performing heinous crimes. Even if by some weird proclivity of fate it was true, why should I get myself embroiled in something a hell of a lot more unpleasant than traffic?

Soon the little old lady was gone and the guy in the pickup truck behind me was honking his horn and spitting tobacco juice. I tooled past the Smokehouse, where I bought my cigars, the Main Book Store, wherein resided Alex the parrot, the post office, from whose steps I'd campaigned for justice of the peace in the manner of Huey P. Long, and Jon Wolfmueller's store, which took care of my somewhat questionable sartorial needs. Kerrville wasn't quite my hometown, I reflected, but neither was New York. My hometown was probably spiritually somewhere between the two, very far away, its longitude and latitude lost in a lullaby. Its citizens were smoke. Its children, beyond any shade of doubt, resided in the trees.

I was daydreaming by the time I pulled into the Butt-Holdsworth Memorial Library parking lot, which is a conducive state of mind if you're going to the library. I'd look through old newspapers for a while. Give the obits a quick scan. Get the hell out of there. If I stayed too long I might stumble on my own name.

The woman behind the counter at the Butt-Holdsworth wasn't Marian the librarian from *The Music Man*, but she maintained roughly the same rigid sense of library decorum. She insisted upon my parking my cigar outside before I had even remembered to whisper. I walked outside, wedged the cigar between two bricks in the wall, and came back in with a micro-chip on my shoulder.

"I'm looking for yesterday's fish wrappers," I said.

"I beg your pardon."

"Back issues of the local rag."

"Just what are you looking for, sir?"

"The croaker section."

"I beg your pardon." She was starting to warm up to me.

"Worm-bait page."

"Are you referring to the obituaries, sir?" She gave a slight moue of distaste.

"Dead right," I said.

In a rather brusque manner the lady pointed me toward the

last row on the far wall. I started to thank her for her help, but she'd already directed her attention to a romance novel being checked out by a woman who greatly resembled a large pelican.

All I could get out of Butt-Holdsworth was a photocopy of the news story about the previous night's victim. It was too late to cover the crime scene and too early for the obit. I mumbled to myself something Uncle Tom often said: "This is *exactly* what I didn't want to happen."

I couldn't find the back issues I was looking for and the lady at the desk had taken on an almost autistic countenance toward me, so I took the photocopy I'd made and picked up my cigar on the way out the door. It was still smoldering. People are rarely as resilient as cigars and most of the time they're a lot less pleasant. Especially when they're lit. I puffed on the cigar like a pneumatic lung for a few moments and pretty soon it was going again and so was I.

Chapter

14

★ ★ ★ ★ ★

The *Kerrville Mountain Sun*, which called itself the "Harvester of Happenings in the Heart of the Hills," was not only somewhat given to the use of alliteration, but had been published once a week for so long it had probably run an obit for Nebuchadnezzar.

J. Tom Graham, the publisher, welcomed me warmly. I told him what I wanted and, before long, I was seated in a dim and dusty back room poring over the ancient newsprint he'd selected for me. As I looked through the obituaries, I thought of some of the things McGovern had told me over the eternal mahogany of a million nocturnal bar conversations. He'd mentioned Alden Whitman, the *Times* obituary writer who had a sixth sense for when people were going to die. When he'd call someone and say "This is Alden Whitman with *The New York Times*," you knew your number was up. Whitman himself had died fairly recently. It wasn't clear whether or not anybody'd called him prior to his departure.

McGovern had written many obituaries for the *Daily*

News. Often they were written when the honoree was still alive. His editor had told him to "Get one in the can" for Hirohito when the Japanese emperor was in the hospital fading fast. McGovern had delivered within twenty-four hours but, unfortunately, the emperor got well. The same thing had occurred with Bob Hope. In fact, anytime McGovern was called upon to write an advance obit for anyone, the subject invariably got better. "Bob Hope's been in the can for ten years," McGovern once told me.

Finding the obits I wanted took little more than an hour out of my life. I figured I could study and compare them like baseball cards later at the ranch. I might very possibly turn up life rafts of survivors and interview them all, but the point, in the final analysis, would most likely be right on top of my head. "Pat Knox be damned," I said, to whatever residual ghosts might be swirling about the little room.

I saddled up Dusty and rode back to the ranch. I walked into the green trailer with a troubled mind and a hand full of death. The cat was sitting in the kitchen sink watching me curiously. The red light on the answering machine was blinking like a panic-stricken whorehouse. Across the small expanse of trailer the red light filtered through the afternoon shadows and pulsed wildly against the ancient, distorted, almost sideshow-like mirror over the sink. It looked like an answering machine from Jupiter. Next to the mirror and directly over the commode a huge, mounted longhorn steer stared malevolently down at me. A hundred years earlier it had peacefully grazed on the prairie until some great white hunter had blown it away. For years it had hung in the lobby of the Bank of Kerrville. Now, since both the steer and the Bank of

Kerrville had gone belly-up, it graced the space immediately above the commode, which required somewhat of an acrobatic maneuver for those who wished to take a Nixon in the trailer. Eons ago, one of its eyes had fallen into the dumper and had never been recovered. The remaining eye appeared to be imploring me to check the answering machine.

I did.

"It's J. Tom Graham," the tape said, "from the *Kerrville Mountain Sun*. Please call me as soon as you get this message."

Some shard of good sense told me not to call J. Tom Graham. Just take the news account of last night's murder—which, I'd noticed, did not mention the victim's lips being sewn shut—put it together with the four obits, and take the little stack of paper up to the Crafts Corral for Eric Roth to make into one of those little Japanese ducks. Whatever weirdness was going on in the Hill Country was none of my business. If I wasn't damn careful it might keep me from having fun at camp.

Under the gun from the steer's eyeball, I punched J. Tom's number. I lit a cigar and took a few puffs as I waited for him to come on the line. The cat watched rather disapprovingly, I thought.

"Kinkster, how are you?" said J. Tom.

"Long time between dreams," I said.

"A dream's why I called you as a matter of fact. Just after you left, an old lady came in. Said her name was Violet Crabb—"

"That's a funny name."

"So's Kinky. Anyway, she said her sister died a few months

back in a house fire near Pipe Creek. Sounded like one of the obits you were looking for, so I thought I'd call you. She thinks her sister was murdered."

"Go on," I said. I felt a prickly sensation on the back of my neck and it wasn't a daddy longlegs.

"Seems her dead sister appeared to her in a dream. She was wearing a white, formal dress and walking toward her. Suddenly, she could see blood dripping from her breast and her side and her neck—"

"Hold the weddin', J. Tom. It's just some old lady's dream. Maybe Violet Crabb had gas or something. Why are you trying to spook me with this?"

"I thought you'd be interested since you were checking up on the same old lady she was dreaming about. The two of you coming in like that was a little too close for coincidence. What's goin' on, Kinkster? You wouldn't be wearing your Sherlock Holmes cap under that cowboy hat, would you?"

"Hell, no, J. Tom. You know I always wear my little yamaha under my cowboy hat. Covers my horns."

"Yeah, well, I've been hearin' some rumors out of the courthouse to the effect that some of the recent deaths around the Hill Country may not have been from natural causes. I checked over some of those obits and there's been a lot of little old ladies droppin' like Texas houseflies around here lately."

I paced back and forth in the trailer, like a tiger tethered to the telephone. I'd been careless letting J. Tom know what I was looking for. Now, whether I got into the case or not, I had a pesky journalist on my hands and in Kerrville it was always a slow day for news.

"Don't believe everything you read in the papers," I said.

"You still want to hear about Violet Crabb's dream?" asked J. Tom relentlessly.

"Spit it."

"Blood's pouring out of her sister and suddenly the white dress goes up in flames. Just before she's totally engulfed in the flames, she whispers one word."

"Plastics?"

Graham laughed a little longer than was necessary. The cat eyed me impatiently.

"What the hell was the word?" I asked.

"Cotillion," he said.

c h a p t e r

★ ★ ★ ★ ★

The next morning I woke up to a nightmare of my own. A Martian was standing in the trailer at my bedside. Each of its eyes was tunneling blinding silver beams of light into my brain. The effect was paralyzing, not to say a bit unnerving. I'd always wanted to be picked up by a UFO, but not before breakfast.

"Kinky," said the Martian. "Wake up!"

I sat up in bed and realized that the Martian was Marilyn and the tunnels of light were the sun's rays reflecting off her thick glasses. On her head, I now observed, was a rather singular silver porpoise-shaped cap that read I SAW SEA WORLD.

Marilyn had, no doubt, left her bunkhouse early, possibly to avoid bunk cleanup, and somehow slipped into my trailer, where she'd stood there like a Martian and scared the hell out of me. Security was pretty lax on the ranch. I, of course, was in charge of security.

Marilyn was what we called a "floater." Someone who didn't necessarily go where they were supposed to go or stay where they were supposed to stay. They tended to cause havoc with bunkhouse counselors, but I felt a certain kinship with them. I'd been a floater most of my life.

We talked about cats and bugs and handicrafts for a while and eventually I aimed her in the direction of her bunkhouse group, put some coffee on, and fed the cat some tuna. While I waited for the coffee to perk I tended to my morning ablutions over the small sink next to the giant steer's head. The eyeball, I noted, was still missing. It was a good thing, too. No matter how well you washed your face or brushed your hair, in the tin, carnival mirror of the green trailer everyone looked like William Henry Harrison.

The sun was doing its best to seep through dusty windows and rusty screens into the bowels of the trailer, but the place still gave off somewhat of a rain forest ambience. I took a cup of coffee, a cigar, the obituary notices, and a rather surly attitude and stepped outside the trailer into the blinding sunlight. A group of young boys, the Mavericks, I believe, came riding by on horseback and waved and shouted. I waved and shouted back.

"Good morning," I said.

"It's afternoon," one kid yelled back.

Still searching for some pattern in the death notices of those little old ladies, I sat down at the shady table behind the trailer and shuffled through them again like a mildly bored riverboat gambler. The victims had nice, old-fashioned names: Virginia, the Bandera bathtub woman; Myrtle, who died in the fire at Pipe Creek and then came back to haunt her sister Violet; Amaryllis, killed by a gunshot near Mountain Home; Prudence, near Kerrville, who'd had a slight reach impediment when it came to her oxygen bottle. I also glanced at the recent news story: Octavia, near Kerrville, who had had her lips sewn together. Had this detail been included, I thought, it was doubtful that the flap, no pun intended, would ever have died down.

There didn't seem to be any link between these cases other than the obvious fact that the victims were all little old ladies. Who could have hated little old ladies that much, I wondered. Maybe the killer was an extremely disgruntled little old man.

The youngest of the women was in her early sixties; the oldest, in her late seventies. They were a surprisingly active group, belonging variously to the Bluebonnet Garden Club, the Lower Turtle Creek Volunteer Fire Department Ladies Auxiliary, the First Methodist Church Vacation Bible Class, the Daughters of the Republic of Texas, the Silver Thimble Quilting Circle, and the Huffers 'n' Puffers Senior Square Dance Club.

Just thinking about all their activities was starting to wear me out. But there seemed to be no pattern here, either. At least nothing you could hook your quilt on. After another cigar and another two cups of coffee, I gave up the ghost on the obits, chucked them inside the trailer, and ankled it up the little hill to the lodge. Sambo, being somewhat myopic, ran toward me barking ferociously, then, at the last moment, smiled like a rat-trap and licked my hand. After studying obits for several hours, a dog licking your hand can almost make you feel good to be alive.

Few heads turned as Sambo and I entered the lodge. Cousin Bucky, who was busy handing rifles out the front door to boys from the Crow's Nest, nodded a brief greeting. Marcie and

Katy were sitting on the couch in the living room locked in an intense meeting with a trio of bunkhouse counselors. Sambo and I slipped past into the back room, where Uncle Tom was at his desk talking on the speakerphone and David Hart, the head men's counselor, was wearing a funny-looking red hat and poring over a computer terminal. Neither looked up.

"Fine," Tom was saying in a tone that indicated the situation was anything but. "That's just *fine*."

"I'm sorry, Dr. Friedman," said the disembodied voice on the speakerphone. "These ice-makers'll get a little hitch in their git-along every now and then—"

"I'm running a camp. I need that machine working now!"

"Well, we may have to order parts—"

"This is *exactly* what I didn't want to happen."

I walked over to where David Hart was working on the evening program.

"Eddie wants to know if you'll sing 'Ol' Shep' for the Hoe-down," he said. "Phallax will be the boy and Eddie will be Ol' Shep and he'll end the song by urinating on both of you from the hidden water bottle like he did last year."

"Smells good from here," I said. "Look, I've got to make a run to town."

David Hart punched in a few things on his computer. "We can spare you," he said.

★

I picked up the obits and a few cigars from the trailer, saddled up Dusty, and headed over to Earl Buckelew's place. Earl was not only a timeless old-timer, he believed that "everything comes out in the wash if you use enough Tide." He'd known the land and the people on the land for so long that he gave directions by the bends of rivers that weren't even there anymore. Maybe he could get inside the minds of these women. If they'd known him when they were younger he might well have broken their hearts.

Earl came out into the yard on a cane, his goats gathering around him like a biblical shepherd. Two severe strokes and the gout had slowed him considerably but they hadn't stopped him. He took me into his house, where the furniture and the pictures on the wall seemed to keep the past alive and the television appeared to run "Wheel of Fortune" on an endless loop.

Earl studied the obituary notices for a long time, slowly shaking his head.

"You don't know any of them?" I asked.

"Don't know *them*," he said, "but I do know widow women. And there's three things you should never try to do. Never try to climb a barbed wire fence leanin' toward you. Never try to kiss a girl leanin' away from you. And never try to get a widow woman to tell you the truth about her age."

I sat back in the rocker, the one that had belonged to Earl's grandfather who'd been captured by the Indians—but that was another story, and one that I didn't wish for Earl to launch into at this time. I thought about the widow women. Of course, they'd all been widows. A small detail maybe, but it might be important.

"How would I get their correct ages?" I asked.

"You could try thinking about a marriage license."

"Earl," I said. "This is so sudden."

Earl laughed. I rocked and thought it over. If I got my ass out of the rocking chair there was still time to get to the courthouse before the Comanches got me. But there was something seductive about Earl's place. Before I knew it, he was telling me about his adventures in Tahiti, which he pronounced in about eleven different ways, pausing only to spit Red Man chewing tobacco into a coffee can on the floor. I rocked comfortably in the chair, smoked my cigar, and listened to the tale I'd heard many times before, almost as if it were a modern mantra. Listening to old people and young people was a hell of a lot better than just listening to middle-aged nerds, I thought. It was certainly better than listening to yourself.

Eventually, Earl wound down and he painfully walked me out to the gate. I thanked him for his help, though I had my doubts about how much light it might shed on the investigation. I was climbing into Dusty when another thought struck me.

"Earl, have you ever heard of a cotillion?"

"Hell," he said, "everybody knows what that is. It's a long-necked lizard from West Texas."

★

A little over an hour later I was standing under a shade tree outside the Kerr County courthouse with five copies of marriage license applications in my hands. Earl Buckelew had been right. The obituaries had been wrong. Almost all of the widow women had lied about their ages.

I took out a pen and small notepad and began doing some

quick calibrations, subtracting the year each woman was born from the year she'd died, which was for all of them the current year. I put my pen and pad away after the first two. It wasn't necessary. The pattern was not only abundantly evident, it was crazier than any you'd be likely to find on a quilt. It made me almost shiver under the shade tree.

Each of the five, at the time of her death, had been exactly seventy-six years old.

Happy Birthday.

Chapter

★ ★ ★ ★ ★

June shed its cocoon; July opened one eye. The summer was rolling obliviously along like a wayward beachball thrown onto the field of a nationally televised sporting event by some California sicko. Over a week had passed since I'd stood on the lawn of the Kerr County courthouse and uncovered a dark secret under the summer sun. I'd kept it to myself. One reason was the horrific nature of some of its possible interpretations. Another reason was that most of the people I talked to these days were about three feet tall. They weren't ready for it yet. I wasn't sure that I was, either.

It was Sunday and I was joining the Bronco Busters' table in the dining hall for lunch. Everyone at the table was seven or eight years old except Ben and Eric, the two counselors, who sat on either side of the little group like enormous bookends. Sunday lunch was always fried chicken and everybody wore their whites. It was Rosie and Elese's fried chicken, but before that it'd been Louise's fried chicken. Before that, long before any of the Bronco Busters had been born, it was Hattie's fried chicken. Before that the chicken had been running around pecking apple cores in the backyard of the Garden of Eden.

The fried chicken was still great and, as always, a big favorite at Echo Hill. Seldom was heard a discouraging word like "cholesterol." As Earl Buckelew once commented: "Hell, when I was growin' up, we didn't even know we had *blood*."

I'd barely laid my hot green peppers out on the table—no Bronco Buster had ever eaten a hot pepper—when the kids began singing the noonday prayer. It was a little number from *Johnny Appleseed* and it went as follows:

> *Oh the Lord is good to me*
> *And so I thank the Lord*
> *For giving me the things I need*
> *The sun and the rain and the appleseed*
> *The Lord's been good to me. Amen. Dig in.*

Eating a fried chicken lunch with a tableful of seven-year-olds will certainly take your mind off weightier matters. Along with the chicken and the mashed potatoes and gravy, the adult world with its ponderous problems just seems to disappear. Conversation is limited to bunkhouse activities, hikes, horses, snakes, water fights, softball, archery, and riflery. The subject of girls never even comes up.

"Is Uncle Tom really your father?"

"Yup."

"And Marcie's your sister?"

"Yup."

"Wow."

"My dad says he was in your bunk when you were ranchers

and that one night you both snuck up and put horse manure in the counselor's bed."

"Very possible."

"Don't get any ideas," said Ben, towering over the table like a giant Buddha.

As I sat amongst the Bronco Busters, a gentle sense of arrested social development came over me. My gaze wandered across the crowded dining hall and my mind wandered back across the hot dusty summers to a time before any of these children were born. I remembered being seven years old myself and watching the oldest boys' bunk playing with their food, mixing it with ketchup and bug juice in a bowl in the middle of the table. Their counselor that summer was an Israeli named Tuvia who'd fought in a number of wars and seen men starve to death in some godforsaken biblical desert. Tuvia took the bowl and three of the culprits away from the dining hall and apparently made them eat the mess, because I vividly remember hearing various retching noises occurring through the choruses as the rest of the ranch was singing a round called "I Like the Flowers." From that day forth I've never had any inclination to play with food.

There were two more things Tuvia did that I would never forget. Once, when the rope snapped during flag lowering and Old Glory fell to the ground with the whole camp standing at mute attention in a circle, Tuvia had snatched it up, put the rope in his teeth, and climbed the old cedar flagpole to tie the rope ends together. I remember thinking that he wasn't even an American.

The other thing Tuvia did was teach us a new bunk yell. It

was almost forty years ago and I still remembered it. The bunk yell went precisely as follows:

> *Avivo! Avavo!*
> *Avivo, vavo, voo-hey!*
> *Lefty, Befty, Billillilla Lefty,*
> *Chingala, Mingala,*
> *Loof, Loof, Loof,*
> *Yea, Bunk Seven!*

That was all in the mid-fifties before the bunks had names. Now Tuvia himself was just a name, remembered only by a very few of us. A member of a lost tribe that wanders somewhere within the soul. Sooner or later all of us would be members of that tribe.

To the boisterous strains of "When They Built the Ship Titanic" I handed my plate and silverware to the ranch KP and slipped out ahead of the throng. I smoked a cigar by the old bell that stood by the office. I looked out at the empty flat soon to be swarming with scores of ranchers. From inside the dining hall the kids were now singing "Happy Birthday" to Eddie Wolff. At the end of the normal birthday song they tagged it with a rather unusual traditional Echo Hill verse. Sung in a minor key in the style of a funeral dirge, it went like this:

> *Happy birthday, happy birthday,*
> *Misery is in the air,*
> *People dying everywhere,*
> *Happy birthday, happy birthday.*

"Not inappropriate," I said to the bell, "considering recent events."

But the bell held its tongue.

Chapter 17

★ ★ ★ ★ ★

Though it was clear to me that five women had been croaked on their seventy-sixth birthday, I was still somewhat disinclined to rush with the news to Pat Knox or Sheriff Kaiser. As far as the J.P. was concerned, a little bit of the little judge went a long way. I didn't want this whole megillah to turn into a Nancy Drew affair with the judge playing Nancy and me in the role of one of her little chums, both of us futilely attempting to operate outside the powers that be. As for Sheriff Kaiser, it was indubitably her attitude that a little bit of Kinky went a long way. It was a hell of an understatement to say that she would not be particularly desirous of entertaining another audience with me. The last one had been a tension convention, the repellent memory of which neither of us was soon likely to forget.

On the other hand, since the day I'd learned that terrible secret on the courthouse lawn, the onus of that dark knowledge had been weighing heavily on my conscience. I now knew beyond any shadow of a doubt that these five deaths could not be written off to coincidence. They were murders—a string, a chain, a cheap imitation necklace strung together by a madman—the end of which was nowhere in sight.

This knowledge pressed brutishly against the translucent butterfly wings of my soul as I flitted in and out of camp activities, my mind always returning to the little old ladies who'd been hastened, if ever so slightly, through death's door. If even one more victim were to be killed while I was the sole possessor of a crucial clue to the murderer's dark agenda it would take a hell of a lot of Tide to make everything come out in the wash.

I puffed on the cigar and wandered the flat on that sunny Sunday afternoon until the singing stopped in the dining hall. After a few moments I heard Uncle Tom's voice saying "Well . . . ?" and answered by an army of children shouting "What are we *waiting* for!" Then the doors of the dining hall flew open and the peaceful little valley was suddenly alive with children running, shouting, and laughing. The hills seemed to echo their energy and joy, and it was a little sad to think how very briefly they would stay this way before joining all the other gray, weatherbeaten souls in the quotidian adult world.

I left my cigar on the ledge and walked into the nearly deserted dining hall, where Uncle Tom was wearing his blue safari hat and working out a chess problem with an eight-year-old boy named Danny. They stood on either side of a huge wooden board I'd bought in Nuevo Laredo in another lifetime. With the chessboard at table level, the king and queen were slightly taller than Danny.

As I stood a little distance away there seemed something rather poignant about the tableau. The innocent intensity of the small boy and the equally intense sincerity of the large man. Chess, like life, is one of those rarest of endeavors that should never be taken lightly. In the case of life, it should, of course, never be taken at all.

"Treat adults like children and children like adults!" I said, quoting Tom after the little tableau had dissolved and Danny had rushed off to buy Cokes with the other kids.

"Why not?" he said to the rows of empty tables and benches. "Almost nothing's ever been accomplished the other way."

"True," I said. "As I'm finding out in this current Kerrville caper."

"What's the latest with Pat Knox's little mystery?"

"It's not really Pat Knox's little mystery."

"Whose is it?"

"I'm not sure. But whoever it is is going to have his or her hands rather full. I think I've stepped on something and it ain't third base. I was going through the marriage license applications down at the courthouse the other day and I discovered that all five victims were seventy-six years old."

"The likelihood of that occurring naturally is statistically very small."

"Tom, they were all killed on their birthdays."

"Sure. Fine. Whatever. Sonny boy, you've got to turn this over to the sheriff. We're running a children's camp here. We can't allow the ranch to become involved with anything like this. We're not equipped to handle it. We're not geared—"

"I'll meet with the sheriff, all right? I'll go into town to-morrow."

David Hart, wearing his funny red hat and carrying a clip-board, wandered into the dining hall just in time to hear my last sentence. He looked down briefly at his clipboard.

"We can spare you," he said.

Even then, on that torpid Monday afternoon in July as I was driving Miss Dusty to Kerrville, some part of my consciousness, some dim forgotten street corner of my peripheral vision, was stirring with the unpleasant notion that the baton pass to Sheriff Kaiser would not entirely extricate me from the ancient rusted meat hook that was this case. Maybe it was a deeper, darker well than a small-town sheriff's department could fathom or plumb. Maybe God, in his divine evenhanded perversity, was watching over all amateur Jewish private investigators and wished them to receive credit for stumbling over vital clues. That was unlikely, I figured, as I smoked a cigar and sped with the top down beneath a canopy of cottonwoods, cypress, and Spanish oak. God had created them, so they'd told me in Sunday school. God had also created a rather tedious situation with me and Sheriff Frances Kaiser. Not that I particularly blamed God. I wasn't even sure if God was a he, she, or it. Possibly, he was the guy on the dim street corner of my peripheral vision who was looking for spare change for a sex change.

Maybe he was none of the above.

"A door is ajar," said Dusty.

"Nice of you to mention it," I said, "but why'd you wait till I was halfway to Kerrville?" I opened the driver's door and slammed it shut again.

"Thank you," said Dusty.

"You're welcome," I said.

As Dusty and I climbed the steep hill between the ranch and Kerrville, I noticed that the sky was growing increasingly foreboding. If you were writing a Victorian novel you might say the clouds were becoming edged with pewter. In Texas, we'd say they were getting dark.

However you described it, the changing weather was only a physical manifestation of what I sensed were deeper, deadlier changes. Changes within the psyche of a killer capable of restraint and of remarkable rage. Changes in a weatherbeaten, war-torn world that was capable of absolutely anything. No big deal. I'd turn my evidence of murder most methodical over to the powers that be. That'd be all she wrote, so I thought. At the time, assuredly, I did not expect the hand of fate to be quite so well manicured. Nor was I aware that it might indeed be clutching quite such a prolific or such a poisoned pen.

Thunder was crashing and lightning was forking the summer sky as I parked Dusty near the courthouse on Earl Garrett Street. The cat, I figured, was probably hiding under the bed in the trailer. She did not particularly like the sound of thunder, and Sambo liked it even less. It wasn't all that popular with me, either, in spite of Ratso's oft-noted contention that thunderstorms produce "negative ionization" which is "psychologically beneficial" to people. Ratso says that pounding surf can produce the same effects as thunderstorms in making you feel more energetic and creative—though, to my knowledge, Ratso's never been near an ocean in his life, having rarely left the confines of Manhattan, which, according to Ratso, is a positive-ion environment conducive to suicide. Ratso also says that rich people often secretly install negative-ion generating machines in all the rooms of their houses, which helps them constantly think up more ways of making money and thereby maintain their wealth.

I asked Ratso once, as I looked around his hideously cluttered apartment, why he hadn't bought a negative-ion generator for his own place. Aside from the obvious reason that there wasn't any room for it. His answer was: "They don't sell 'em on Canal Street."

I walked patiently, luxuriantly through the storm to the courthouse and shook the rain off my cowboy hat into a nearby spittoon. The halls were dark, and so was the look on the secretary's face when I told her I had to see the sheriff but I didn't have an appointment.

"Always make an appointment if you want to see the sheriff," said the secretary. "She's got a very busy schedule and she hardly ever sees anyone without an appointment."

"I'll write that down in my Big Chief tablet," I said.

Considerably later, and much to the secretary's surprise, I found myself looking across the big desk at Sheriff Kaiser. I don't know whether or not the sheriff had a negative-ion generator going for her but the room certainly had an almost palpable negative atmosphere. The secretary left and closed the door behind her.

"What do you want?" said the sheriff.

"Not a thing," I said. "Just have a look at these."

In a manner roughly akin to Bret Maverick, I fanned out the five copies of the marriage license applications on the desk before the sheriff.

"What're these?" she said.

"Five of a kind."

As Frances Kaiser adjusted her glasses and picked up the documents I walked over to the window and watched the storm. I lit a cigar and watched the trees on the courthouse lawn sway with an almost violent grace like dancers in Borneo. I imagined the emotions that must've been traversing the sheriff's face as she read. Doubt, astonishment, thinly veiled anger. I was sure she'd been working diligently to get the grand jury seated, possibly prodding the D.A. to get his case together in order to gain an indictment against the suspect still in custody. The man she believed had sewn an old lady's lips together. Now all that might be out the window. Into the storm.

Once the forces of the law are set into motion, once the D.A. goes for an indictment, the grand jury almost invariably rubber-stamps his recommendation. As Rambam once said: "If the D.A. really wanted it, the grand jury would indict a couch." But now the forces of the law in this little town might have to take a step backward and rethink things a bit. Outside

the window the forces of nature continued wild and un-
abated. They were not influenced by the D.A.'s recommendation. They were not subject to the sheriff's authority. They did
seem to be moderately interested in exactly how far they
could propel a deputy's straw cowboy hat across the courthouse lawn and down Main Street.

"I see," said the sheriff, as she stared past the window out
into the fury of the storm. Her face was an emotionless porce-
lain mask that in some strange way seemed more unnerving
than any display of mere emotion. I puffed politely on the
cigar and waited.

"You obtained these documents—"

"Down the hall," I said. "But it was Earl Buckelew's idea to
check the marriage license applications."

"Ol' Earl," said the sheriff, her eyes going back in time.
"We used to sneak onto his place and go fishin' when I was a
kid."

"The same. He claims widow women always lie about their
ages."

Sheriff Kaiser smiled. It was a nice smile. Sheriffs usually
don't get to smile a lot but when they do it's always appreci-
ated. Kind of like Ronald Reagan giving a turkey to an orphanage on Thanksgiving.

The sheriff stood up, got rid of the smile, and stacked the
pages neatly on her desk. It was a gesture of dismissal and I
edged toward the door.

"You've been a good citizen," she said. "We'll take it from
here."

"I just did what anybody would do."

"If that was really true," she said, "I'd be out of a job."

I opened the door and headed for the hallway.

"One more thing," the sheriff called after me.

I turned around. She was standing like a giant in the doorway.

"Tell Earl Buckelew that one of the little Kaiser girls said hello."

Chapter

★ ★ ★ ★ ★

It was around eleven that night when the phone rang in the green trailer. Pam Stoner, the green-eyed handicrafts counselor from Oklahoma, and I were getting acquainted on a big flat rock out back. We had a Roy Rogers blanket that had somehow survived the lifetime of childhood and a few shots of Jack Daniel's with a little Mr. Pibb backing it up. The cat was watching from the roof of the trailer.

"I'd better take this call," I said.

"You really *are* Jewish," said Pam Stoner.

"The ugly head of anti-Semitism rears up out of a peaceful, bucolic setting," I said, as I, too, reared up and moved toward the trailer.

"Bring the bottle with you when you come back," she said. She was smiling and her star-colored eyes seemed to be shimmering in the moonlight. A whippoorwill was calling from a nearby juniper tree. Maybe that should've been the call I took.

I grabbed the bottle with one hand and took the persistent blower from its cradle with the other.

"Syrian Embassy," I said.

"This is Pat Knox," said the blower, "returning your call. I already know what happened at the sheriff's office today, so you don't need to fill me in on that. You done good."

"Thanks, Your Honor. Looks like the sheriff now realizes these five deaths are related."

"Gettin' her to realize it is only half the battle. The other half is gettin' her to do somethin' about it."

"She assured me the full force of the law will be behind the case."

Pat Knox laughed. It was a long, hearty, bitter laugh. When she recovered, her tone was dangerous and conspiratorial in nature.

"You and I have sure put her on the right track, but if you'll pardon the choice of words, this case may just be too kinky for the sheriff."

"It may be too kinky for me, too." I twisted the top off the bottle of Jack and took a short pull.

"That's not quite true," said the judge. "And if there's one thing I know about you it's that you've got the kind of mind that loves a good mystery."

I looked out the back window of the trailer and saw Pam lying on her back on the big rock in a very suggestive position.

"That's right, Judge. Me and Miss Marple love a good mystery. What've you got?"

"Come see for yourself. You're not gonna quit on me, are you? Let that big ol' sheriff scare you?"

The big ol' sheriff didn't scare me. In fact, she'd turned in a rather poignant performance that afternoon. But there was something almost sirenlike in Pat Knox's appeal. And I wasn't referring to the thing that's mounted on the top of police cars.

I looked out the window and saw that nothing was going to be mounted around the ranch that night. Pam was asleep on the rock.

"Okay," I said. "Where do we meet?"

"Midnight. The Garden of Memories."

"The cemetery?"

"Boo!" said Pat Knox, and she hung up.

Chapter

20

★ ★ ★ ★ ★

If you've got to go to a bone orchard, midnight's about as good a time as any. Things are just beginning to get stirring and you avoid the crowds. It was a funny thing, but the closer I got to the cemetery the more I felt drawn to it. Sort of like a part-time ghoul returning to the crypt. Of course, all ghouls are pretty much part-time. Being a ghoul twenty-four hours a day would kill anybody. Such were my thoughts as I drove up to the gates of the Garden of Memories. One other little thought that was in my mind was that Sheriff Kaiser probably wouldn't approve of whatever Judge Knox and I were going to be doing here. But who was afraid of the big ol' sheriff?

I hooked a right off Sidney Baker Street and urged Dusty slowly through the main entrance to the bone orchard. The place was quieter even than the Butt-Holdsworth Memorial Library. Between the two of them there'd been a lot of books and a lot of people checked out. But there was no one here to say "Ssshhhh . . ." Only the wind whispering in the shadows of the willow trees.

There didn't seem to be any human forms moving around or any vehicles parked along the entrance road. I drove a little farther until the town of Kerrville had disappeared behind me and the bone orchard had pretty well swallowed me up. It was not an entirely unpleasant sensation. There was a certain sense of peace to it. Kind of like the way it must feel to be inside a McDonald's after closing time. Of course, there was no closing time here. There was not even any time here. It didn't at the moment particularly feel like there was any here here.

So I hit the brights.

Dark forms and figures began springing up all over the graveyard. Dripping half-shadows of passengers aboard the *Titanic* descended from the willow branches. A partially drawn shade of Ichabod Crane galloped by with hooves of distant thunder. Cowboys and Indians and Jews and gypsies and homosexuals and tiny little Cambodians and soldiers and sailors and airmen from wars that are now trivia questions leapt up out of the night in the manner of game show contestants with the answers to the mysteries of life. But none of them spoke a word. Imagination can be a blessing, I thought, but it can also be pretty tedious.

I puffed my cigar nervously.

Dusty shuddered.

Then, off to the side, glowing darkly through the night with the ageless intensity of Anne Frank's eyes, came a beacon no less welcome than had it shone down from the Old North Church or skipped softly across the waters that gently lapped at Daisy Buchanan's pier.

Then the light vanished along with any residual personal enjoyment I had at being in that particular locus at that particular time. I pulled Dusty over to the side of the little road, not that there was a lot of oncoming traffic, and waited. The light did not come on again.

I got out of the car, performed a few square-dance maneuvers around the headstones, and, following the directions of an old Bob Dylan song, "walked ten thousand miles in the miles of a graveyard." I bumped into an ill-placed tombstone and almost burned my forehead. Recovering my balance I took stock of the desolate landscape. Where the light had been there was nothing. All around me in every direction there was nothing. It was like the sensation you sometimes get when you're standing in the middle of a busy shopping mall.

I stared up at the scythelike moon and the little freckling of stars and tapped a cigar ash onto the ground.

"Ashes to ashes," I said.

"I wouldn't be so sure of that," said a voice that scared the shit out of me.

I landed a few moments later, practically impaling myself upon a small wooden cross. I struggled to my feet, glanced at the cross, and then at Judge Knox.

"It's a good thing it wasn't one of those pointy-headed stars of David," I said.

"There are *some* advantages to living in Kerrville," she said.

"And dying in Kerrville," I said. "A lot of people seem to be doing it. By the way, why are we here?"

"Follow me," she said.

As I trudged behind the little judge and her shining path through the darkened country graveyard, no elegies came to mind. The only things that popped up were more shades, more shadows, more questions, the primary one from the latter category still being: "What the hell are we doing here?"

Finally, we reached an area in the back of the cemetery in which this season's crop appeared to have been recently planted. The ground looked fresh, there were more flowers, and the stones were new enough to gleam slightly in what moonlight there was. These were definitely not the kind of stones that gather no moss. They'd soon be gathering plenty of it, along with litter, lichens, birdshit, and, conceivably, the occasional teenage swastika. Like many of the living, these stone faces seemed resigned to whatever fate lay before them.

"Three of our little ladies are buried here," said the judge. "The second victim, Myrtle Crabb, got burned up in the fire at Pipe Creek. They just went ahead and cremated her."

"Might as well dance with who brung you."

"Her son, I understand, drives around with her ashes on his motorcycle."

"Every mother's dream."

"The fourth victim, Prudence South, the one who needed the oxygen bottle, she's buried in a little church cemetery out the other side of town. So that leaves victims one, three, and five buried here. C'mon, I'll show you."

The judge walked like a determined little rooster to a plot about thirty feet away. I followed faithfully, puffing on my faithful cigar and beginning to realize that Judge Knox was either pulling a somewhat premature Halloween prank by bringing me here or she was really onto something.

"Here's Virginia. Supposedly drowned in the tub in Bandera."

She had a nice shiny granite stone. On the grave itself was

one yellow rose. Pat Knox turned and I followed her farther into the graveyard.

"Amaryllis," she said. "Supposedly shot herself."

"In the back of the head. Wouldn't that be difficult?"

"For a seventy-six-year-old arthritic little lady, damn near impossible."

Amaryllis had a smaller, more modest stone. There was a vase of wilting flowers on the grave. Beside the vase were three yellow roses.

"Come along," said the judge.

I stepped around and over the macabre obstacle course and followed her to the other side of the recently planted section. The night seemed to have gotten a good bit chillier and there was a fog rolling in from somewhere. There weren't any oceans around. Where was the fog coming from, I wondered. Possibly, all bone orchards get a little misty after midnight. Who's to say that they don't?

"Octavia," said a voice out of the fog.

I remembered Octavia. Her lips had been sewn together. Not an item you easily forget. I walked around the grave. The marker was a stone cross. There was a scroll on a little pedestal acknowledging her as an active lifetime member of the Daughters of the Republic of Texas. On the grave were six yellow roses.

"Six yellow roses," I said. "Either somebody's made a floral typo or we're missing one of our little ladies."

"This person's pretty meticulous. I think if we hunt around a little we'll find there's been a victim we've overlooked."

"When did you first notice the flowers?"

"I've been checking some vandalism in this cemetery the

past few days. The flowers weren't on the graves when I came by late this afternoon. Somebody put 'em here tonight."

"Looks like I'm drawn to this case whether I like it or not. I'm trapped like an insect in amber. You win, Judge."

"I knew you'd see things my way," she said, smiling a slightly cadaverous smile.

"Since you've got the contacts and the resources," I said, "why don't you try to locate our missing victim?"

"I'll do that," she said. "What are you going to be doing?"

I puffed on the cigar and blew a little smoke into the foggy night.

" 'There's a yellow rose of Texas,' " I said, " 'that I am going to see.' "

21

★ ★ ★ ★ ★

Bright and early the next morning after I'd delivered a Gandhi-like truckload of ranch laundry to a nice lady named Arlena at the Country Clean Laundromat, I went to the Del Norte Restaurant for breakfast. Huevos rancheros without the yolks—my one healthy-heart habit. Chain-smoke Hoyo de Monterrey Rothschilds Maduros, drink as much Jameson's as Gram Parsons drank tequila in the last few months of his life, and always eat huevos rancheros without the yolks if your waitress speaks enough English to get your order right, and you'll live forever. Your life may not be very pleasant, but you can't have everything. You've got to decide what it is you really want, ninety-seven years of shit or Mozart?

It was still not yet eight in the morning and I was walking in the alleyway between the parking lot and the stores on Earl Garrett Street quietly cursing Ben Stroud. Ben had convinced Uncle Tom that the riflery program at camp had reached such a fever pitch that Ben himself must be present to supervise the qualifications. This left me to do the early morning laundry run and David Hart, Eddie, or Wayne the Wrangler to take the midafternoon run. The advantage to the early morning laundry run was that it was over fast, like a number of love affairs I'd been involved in. By seven forty-five I was through for the day.

Most of the stores didn't open till nine, but I thought I heard some activity inside Wolfmueller's Town and Country Clothiers. I knocked on the back door.

"Who is it?" said a muffled voice.

"Charles Starkweather," I said.

I pushed the door open. Over about eight rows of tuxedos on movable floor racks I could barely make out Jon Wolfmueller's head. He looked up from his invoices and calculator, waved me in, and returned to his work.

"Who's Charles Starkweather?" he said.

"How soon they forget. Got any coffee?"

"Right over there on the other side of the discontinued styles rack."

"Jesus Christ. How can you have discontinued styles in Kerrville?"

Jon was busily at work back at the invoices and did not respond. I sipped some coffee and paced between the racks of clothes.

"Just wait'll the Nehru jacket hits town," I said. "That'll create a buzz."

Jon paid no attention. I sipped more coffee.

"Jon," I said, "I need your help with something."

"I don't have any openings for male models, if that's what you're hinting at."

Jon did have a sense of humor lurking back there somewhere. I often, in fact, referred to him as my faithful Indian companion. He wasn't an Indian, of course. Tied to the store as he was, he didn't even make much of a companion. But good help was hard to get these days for both of us. Jon was one of the few Kerrverts I knew who seemed to enjoy my company. At least he put up with me for extended periods of time. Maybe he *was* an Indian.

One thing was for sure. Jon knew what was going on in Kerrville, and anything Jon didn't know, his wife, Sandy, who ran Pampell's drugstore and soda fountain, most assuredly did. Between the two of them I had my finger on the sometimes rather shallow pulse of Kerrville. I knew others, of course. Jody Rhoden, the photographer. Max Swafford, my former campaign manager, who abandoned the campaign right in the middle of the race to search for a gold mine in Mexico. Dylan Ferrero, who'd moved to Kerrville recently from a little town called Comfort, Texas, and communicated almost entirely in rock 'n' roll lyrics. When you're trying to keep a low profile and not irritate the sheriff, personal contacts were the only way to go. And Jon Wolfmueller was the place to start.

"Jon," I said, "what do you know about this grand jury they're convening about the woman who was murdered and had her lips sewn together?"

Jon pursed his lips in an unconscious manner not dissimilar to the way the victim must've appeared and thought it over. I sipped more coffee.

"I know they're having a hard time getting the grand jury together for some reason. I know the sheriff and the justice of the peace are each about ready to kill the other and sew her lips together. I don't know the name of the subject of the grand jury."

"That's kept secret."

"Don't bet on it. Why don't you go on over and ask Sandy?"

I headed down Earl Garrett and hung a right on Water Street till I reached Pampell's Drug Store, a building that had once belonged to the legendary Singin' Brakeman, Jimmie Rodgers, the man most people credit for popularizing the guitar in America. Rodgers was a seminal country blues singer who, next to Elton Britt, was the greatest yodeler of his time or anybody else's. Jimmie wasn't around anymore. He'd died of TB in New York City when most of us were jumping rope in the schoolyard. But every time I went into Pampell's and looked up at the old balconies that had once surrounded his music hall and recording studio, I could hear a little distant Dopplered echo of a train whistle.

Sandy was setting up the soda fountain. There was already one customer, a skinny old man wearing a straw hat and a bolo tie.

"Jon just called," she said. "You wanted to know who's the subject of the grand jury?"

"I thought they were supposed to keep his identity secret."

Sandy laughed. "There's never been a secret in Kerrville that everybody didn't know," she said.

"It's one of them funny-soundin' Mescan names," offered the old man. "Rod-*ree*-gis. Gui-*tar*-is. One of them hard-to-say kind of names."

"The guy's name is Garza," Sandy told me.

The old man nodded his head and cackled softly to himself. "*Gar*-za," he said. "There's a jawbreaker."

22

★ ★ ★ ★ ★

I got a cup of coffee from Sandy and she vanished to the back of the store. I decided to kill a little time and pain there at the old soda fountain until nine o'clock, when the Rose Shop just across Sidney Baker Street opened up. There were only three or four florists in Kerrville. If I was going to get a lead on who'd bought the yellow roses it wasn't going to take very long. That was one advantage to being in a small town when it came to crime solving. It was the reason Miss Jane Marple, arguably Agatha Christie's greatest detective, chose to live in St. Mary Mead instead of London. Jane Marple and Agatha Christie, I reflected as I sipped my coffee, were little old ladies themselves.

Jane Marple, of course, would live forever in the timeless casino of fiction, waiting for the freckled, feckless hand of a young person in Wyoming to pluck her off some dusty shelf and fall in love with the mysteries of life. Agatha Christie, like Jimmie Rodgers, wasn't around anymore but in a sense I suppose they both still were, for they continued to ply silent rivers of words and music down into the yawning rugosities of our lives. Silver threads in an otherwise drab embroidery. Too bad Jimmie and Agatha never met. Might've made an interesting couple.

"If it don't rain again by the tenth of July," the old man with the bolo tie was saying, "then it ain't gonna rain for the whole summer. It's gonna be a hell of a scorcher."

"Even if it does rain," I said, as I laid down a buck for my coffee, "it's not going to be too pleasant."

Jesus Christ, I thought. Here I was casually paying a buck for a cup of coffee. What was the world coming to? We dressed casually. Waved casually on the street. Nobody got too excited. Everybody went with the flow. Now some nerd had casually taken six little old ladies off the board.

"Boll weevil's comin' back again," said the old-timer as I headed for the door.

"Ain't we all, brother," I said.

★

At approximately 9:01 A.M. I crossed Sidney Baker Street and entered the Rose Shop, where an irritating little bell rang just above the door and climbed halfway into my inner ear. There was a fairly wide selection of flowers. The flowers smiled at me and I smiled back at them. No one else was in sight. No yellow roses, either.

"Someone in Texas Loves You," read a bright ceramic wall hanging. "God Loves You," read a nearby colorfully painted plate.

"Make up your mind," I said.

"Can I help you?" said a voice from above.

This is it, I thought. On a bumper sticker, vengeance is mine saith the Lord. The family of man might be fairly dysfunctional but now God was coming down to straighten things out. And She did sound slightly irritated.

I looked up and saw a rather nice pair of legs descending a ladder. The legs were attached to a lady who was holding a hanging plant. She looked pretty earthy for a florist.

Her name, I soon learned, was Betty and she knew a lot about flowers. A little more, possibly, than I wanted to know.

But she didn't have any yellow roses.

"Sometimes we'll go months without selling any yellow roses. We haven't sold any in a long while. Now June through August we do have available our special 'Texas Dozen' offer. That's fifteen flowers for $29.95."

"But no yellow roses?"

"Red."

"But if I wanted yellow, could you get them?"

"We'd have to order them. We'd bring them in from Austin or San Antonio. It might take a few days. Stores don't usually stock them."

"How long will roses last once you sell them?"

"Well, that depends. Outdoors, indoors. Air conditioning, no air conditioning. Drafts will kill 'em faster than anything. Never put your roses in a draft."

"Thanks for the tip."

Betty seemed to be working up a bit of a second wind herself.

"Now once we sell 'em we'll only guarantee 'em for twenty-four hours. If something happens to 'em within twenty-four hours you can just bring 'em right back to us and we'll see that they're replaced. If it's after twenty-four hours, you're on your own."

"Got to be tough."

"Did you want the Texas Dozen?"

"I'm not sure."

"Only $29.95."

"I don't know," I said. "I'm kind of like James Taylor. I just can't remember who to send 'em to."

"Well, you've got to the end of August."

"That's a relief."

★

I thanked Betty and cut buns out of there. I got in the old gray pickup and headed out toward Ingram, to a place called Showers of Flowers. I dimly recalled buying some roses there several lifetimes ago and sending them to a long-distance lover who worked at a Cadillac dealership in Spokane. She'd sent me a nice note back. Though it was addressed "Dear Occupant," I'd still thought the relationship worth pursuing. Of course, it wasn't, she wasn't, and at the time, from most accounts, I probably wasn't either. But it is precisely this futility, pain, and seeming absence of true communication that keep the flower shops of the world in business and, every once in a while, when shaken slightly, may even envelop the stars. Maybe I should've sent her a Texas Dozen.

Showers of Flowers was a big down-home kind of place

with several greenhouses out back and flowers of every variety under the sun, so to speak. I saw the yellow roses right away. The owner, a friendly guy named Al, saw me right away.

"I remember the first time you bought flowers here," he said. "A long time ago when we first opened up."

"Spokane?"

"Before Spokane. Even before Los Angeles."

The guy was weaving a spiderweb of heartbreak right before my eyes. "It was to Hawaii. A dozen beautiful red roses in a very nice ornate vase, as I recall. You haven't forgotten?"

It had been a long time ago. The flowers had been for Kacey, who'd died very young and been pressed between the pages of my life more than a decade ago. I'd called the hotel in Maui to make sure the flowers had gotten there. Kacey'd already left for Vancouver but I still recalled the words of the maid who was cleaning up the room. "The lady leave the vase," she'd said, "but she take the flowers."

"I haven't forgotten," I said.

I steered the conversation gently to yellow roses.

"How many yellow roses do you sell, Al?"

"I don't sell roses. People buy them. Yellow roses are very popular in Texas. For a friend, somebody in the hospital. Red is for deep love and things like that. We also have pink, white, and sonya. We grow 'em ourselves. We've got our own greenhouses here."

"What's sonya?"

"Between pink and orange. Very pretty. We go through fifteen to twenty dozen roses a week. You always bought red before. Why do you want yellow?"

"I got a friend in the hospital who doesn't like pink or white. Really hates sonya."

After some little badgering, my insistence upon the urgency of the matter, and my promise to treat with some semblance of confidentiality the relationship between a man and his florist, I got Al to bud a little. He'd sold yellow roses to three people over the past week. Or rather, they'd bought them. Al was understandably hesitant to show me the invoices with the customers' names and addresses.

"I can't tell you why I need this information, Al, but it's very important to me. In its own way, it means as much as Spokane, Los Angeles, and even Hawaii. And if I'm not being too melodramatic, lives may be at stake."

Al was a trusting sort. He let me copy the invoices. Names, addresses, dates. He also directed me to the other two remaining florists in the area. I thanked him and hoped to hell the flowers someone had placed in the Garden of Memories weren't purchased out of town.

The third florist was closed. On vacation since the week before. So I drove across town to the last flower shop on my list. That was another advantage to a small town, I thought. You could drive all the way across it in less time than it took to find a cab in New York. And you could smoke a cigar without anybody giving you grief.

Hitting all the flower shops in Kerrville was the kind of investigative work Rambam would've liked. The life of the real P.I., he'd always contended, was made up of ninety-eight percent boring routine bullshit. The other two percent, he'd added, was merely tedious. According to Rambam, most of the time the results of long hard hours of digging in the investigative field would be inconclusive. Most cases, especially serial murders, were solved through dumb luck. Ted Bundy forgetting to fix his taillight. Jeffrey Dahmer repeatedly calling his refrigerator repair man.

The last place turned out to be a small affair on Ace Ranch Road just across the way from the Veterans Cemetery, which is a good location if you're a flower shop. The fellow who ran it was a baby-faced, middle-aged guy who looked like he was wearing one of Jon Wolfmueller's discontinued styles. There was nothing yellow in the store except his teeth.

"You don't have any yellow roses, do you?" I said. It was pretty obvious he didn't.

"We sure don't. We've got some nice summery arrangements, if you'd like that. I could get you some yellow roses, but it may take a day or two."

"Well, I'll tell you what I'd really like. I think someone may have ordered some yellow roses from here recently. Would you have any information on that?"

He looked at me curiously for a moment. Then he smiled. It was not a nice smile. Obviously I wasn't going to be any florist's favorite customer.

"Let me check," he said, and he disappeared into the back of the shop.

I waited. After a while I wondered if he'd passed away. Eventually he returned with a scrap of paper and my patience was rewarded.

"I don't know why you need this, buddy, but I can't see as it does anybody any harm. They were delivered here." He handed me the paper with a name and address on it.

"Thanks," I said. "You've been a great help."

"You ain't with the CIA, are you?" He laughed a loud, high-pitched, dangerous, redneck laugh. He laughed and laughed.

I laughed, too.

Then I left.

I figured if the case was going to be solved by dumb luck, I might as well strike while the iron was hot. I had the names and addresses of the four local people who'd purchased yellow roses within the past week. Why not run them down right now? There was an outside chance I could wrap this unsavory little booger up in a sailor's knot before lunchtime, dump the whole thing on Sheriff Kaiser's desk, and she'd pat the top of my cowboy hat and tell me what a good citizen I was. There was also an outside chance that she would become mildly agitato and have me committed to the Bandera Home for the Bewildered.

I checked the first address from Al at Showers of Flowers and gunned the old gray pickup down the road in that direction. Soft drink cans, basketballs, and old .177 rifles recently used in a tableau of Ira Hayes at Iwo Jima slid back and forth across the bed of the truck, making a hell of a racket under the attached camper. I shot a quick backward glance through the window of the cab and saw a sea monster swirling around back there, trying to reach through and grab my throat. A lit cigar fell out of my mouth as I hurtled down the highway. I wasn't sure if it'd fallen on the seat between my legs or on the floor, where it'd probably roll under the seat and most likely burn me to death.

"Mother of God," I said nervously. "This is what I live for." A truck loaded with bales of hay barreled by on my right at about ninety-seven miles an hour.

Without taking my eyes off the highway I rose up slightly in the saddle and frantically felt around between my legs. Nothing was there except what was supposed to be, but I did receive a dirty look from a lavender-haired lady in a late-model Buick. Then I turned my attention to the sea monster. It was an old tennis net with fresh seaweed from the waterfront threaded all through it. King Neptune had worn it the week before on Shipwreck Night. Then I found a place to pull off to the side of the road, got out, and felt around under the seat until I burned the shit out of my hand.

All in a day's work, I thought. Sometimes it requires pawn-shop balls for a private eye to stay on the case.

At a little after eleven I pulled up in front of the first address, a picturesque little house with an actual swear-to-God white picket fence in front of it. It wouldn't have surprised me if some very sick bastard lived there.

A guy who looked like Methuselah's older brother was mowing the lawn on the side of the house with a manual lawn mower. I got out of the truck and walked over to the guy without a thought in my head as to who to tell him I was or what in the hell I was doing there. I decided to settle on the old salesman's icebreaker.

"Good morning, sir. I'm John Wisteria from Florists International. Just checking up on how the roses are doing."

"They're doin' just fine," he said. "They're settin' inside in the air conditionin' and I'm out here mowin' the goddamn lawn."

"You want to be careful with that air conditioning," I said. "A draft can kill them faster than anything."

He looked at me as if he suspected that there was a draft between my ears. "You don't say," he muttered. "What'd you say your name was?"

"Well, I'm just checking," I said, as I wrote a little imaginary note in my notebook. "Just to make sure the yellow roses arrived here all right."

"Of course they arrived here all right. I went to the damn florist and bought 'em. Then I brought 'em home. Gave 'em to my wife for our fifty-seventh anniversary." He was becoming increasingly belligerent.

"That's nice," I said. I began heading back to the truck, but now he wouldn't let me go and began screaming for his wife.

The woman struggled out onto the porch, against my protestations, and backed up her husband on every tedious detail about the yellow roses. She was a grizzled old thing who got around slowly and painfully with one of those aluminum Jerry Jeff Walkers. Her name was Marsupial or something and she was a little deaf, so the dialogue between the two of them went on interminably. If I was the kind of private eye who carried a gun I probably would've pulled it out right there and shot myself to contain my ennui. Eventually, I departed with all three of us shaking our heads in disgust and confusion, softly invoking the names of our various gods.

The visit to my next customer was fast, and required no dis-
sembling on my part. Two moving vans were parked in front
of what looked as if it might've once been a happy home. The
moving men were loading his things into one truck and hers
into the other. The yellow roses were in front of the house,
too. In a trash bin.

There's a million stories in the city, I thought. Who the hell's
to say there's not also a few in the town?

I drove to the third address. On the way I stopped for a cup
of coffee and called Pat Knox's office from a pay phone. We
agreed to meet for a low-profile lunch at a funky little Mexican restaurant that had a lot of black velvet art going for it
and no clientele from city hall.

When I got to the third address I was not surprised. It was
the hospital. Just like Al had said, yellow roses for the friend
in the hospital. But I had to be sure. So I checked with the
desk, went up to the fourth floor, asked directions from a
nurse, and walked by the room of a woman in a hospital bed
watching *Smokey and the Bandit*. The yellow roses were there
by the bed. Drooping a little, but so was Burt Reynolds'
cookie-duster. I was oh-for-three in my horticultural area.
The last customer could wait till after lunch. One thing about
dumb luck. You can't force it.

When I sat down at the little corner table at the little Mexican restaurant across from the little judge, I could tell she was
in a more upbeat mood than I was. Sylvia Plath was in a more
upbeat mood than I was.

"What a team," she whispered, almost shimmering with
excitement.

"I don't know," I said. "There're some people—possibly

cases of arrested development—who maintain an interest in high school sports well into their adult years. For them the prospect of going to State is like a lighthouse to their lives. As for me, the prospect of going to State—"

"I'm talking about *us*, you bullethead. *We're* the team."

"—is not as important as the prospect of going to the men's room."

I did have to urinate like a racehorse. But I had another motive for getting up and leaving the table that Judge Knox was not privy to. I wanted to check out the restaurant, the little hallway, and the men's room for any large, burly sheriff's deputies that might report our little rendezvous to Frances Kaiser. I wasn't paranoid or anything. The fact that I was beginning to operate with a mindset not dissimilar to that of the Spy Who Came in from the Cold did not worry me too much.

I returned to the table, sat down, and stared intently at the judge.

"Jabber," I said.

"I've found another seventy-six-year-old woman who died on her birthday. Happened about twenty miles from here in Center Point. Death was ruled accidental."

"This is crazy. We're working practically undercover. The sheriff's doing her thing. The newspapers haven't got anything more than rumors around the courthouse to work with, so they haven't broken the story. And meanwhile, some fiend has pulled the plug on six little old ladies and God knows when or if he's ever going to stop."

"If the papers get hold of this—and they will—there'll be a panic no one's seen the likes of since the Boston Strangler. It's up to us, Richard."

"That's what I was afraid you were going to say." I poked desultorily at my *carne guisada*. "But I love it when you call me Richard."

"What about the yellow roses?" quizzed the judge. "What'd you find out this morning?"

"That only four purchases of yellow roses have been made in this area in the past week or so. Three of them I've accounted for. The fourth came from that little shop near the Veterans Cemetery. I thought I'd check it out after lunch. They were sent to this address."

I handed Pat Knox the last name and address on the list. She studied the scrap of paper.

"This address isn't far from here. There's several old-age homes in that area. Could be one of them."

"We'll both probably be in an old-age home before we solve this case," I said.

"I'm goin' with you to this address," said the judge. She stood up and it seemed likely that lunch was over.

"Only if you promise me a round of croquet," I said.

Chapter

24

★ ★ ★ ★ ★

There didn't seem to be a lot of activity as the judge parked
her car by the side entrance of the Alpine Village Retirement
Center. Of course, there was probably never a lot of activity
around the Alpine Village Retirement Center. It wasn't exactly the best place to go if you wanted to raise some hell.

"Looks quiet as the grave," I said, as we got out of the car.

"Looks can be deceiving," said the judge. "Otherwise, why
would ninety-five percent of the marriages I've performed
lately end in divorce or worse?"

"What's worse than divorce?"

"You'd have to ask the other five percent."

"Jesus," I said, as I carefully placed my lit cigar on a nearby
windowsill. "Almost makes me glad I'm still a closet hetero-
sexual."

As we opened the door and walked from the sweltering
summer afternoon into the side wing of the place it felt like
we'd just taken up residence in the freezer department of a
meat-packing plant.

"If I'd known we were going to Ice Station Zebra," I said, "I'd've worn my long johns."

"Shush," said the judge rather violently.

The hallway was strangely quiet and empty. The only figures we passed were a young black orderly pushing what looked like a scarecrow in a wheelchair. You couldn't tell if the scarecrow was a man or a woman or living or dead. About the only thing you could say for it was it sure kept the crows off the wheelchair.

My mind drifted back to when my father and I saw Doc Phelps for the last time. It was at the state hospital near Silver Spring, New Mexico. Marcie had visited him a few years earlier, before they'd put him in. She'd told me he was very thin and fragile and looked like Rip Van Winkle lying in his bed with storm clouds swirling all around his little house. He'd said that Hilda's ghost had been nagging him about weeding the garden. Then Doc had told Marcie: "I'm a very lucky man because I've loved many people in my life and I still do." Marcie said she'd sat by the side of his bed and cried.

By the time Tom and I saw Doc he'd been at the hospital for a while, been seated next to screaming people eating with plastic silverware, been pushed around like a sack of potatoes by young orderlies who didn't know or care that in the thirties Doc with his pretty young wife on the back of his motorcycle had driven all the way from New York to San Francisco. I'd lifted Doc's birdlike legs one at a time and put him into the front seat of the car as we took him to a restaurant for lunch. He'd smiled at me like a little child through the window, the man who'd led so many of us up the hills and down the canyons of summertime and childhood itself. At the restaurant Doc appeared to slip in and out of lucidity, somewhat in the manner of my own normal conversational style. I was yapping about Santa Monica, California, about people sitting on park benches by the sea and old folks playing shuffleboard. I said there were a lot of crazy, highly creative people out there because you could stand on the edge of the cliff and look out over the sea at night and realize that you couldn't run any farther, that that was as far as you could go.

"Hardly," Doc said. It was one of his more lucid moments.

Doc then proceeded to tell as a recurring theme through the remainder of the meal a story or joke about a woman and the gorilla at the London Zoo. Now that I think back on it, whether the rambling narrative was a story or a joke seems kind of important because Doc was one of the kindest, wisest men I've ever known and his words might've shed some light on whether life is a story or a joke. But life, like an orderly, was pushing me along too fast to remember what he said, and now it's too late to ask him to tell me again.

On the way back to the hospital that day, Doc seemed to become disoriented. Tom asked him if he knew where we were. Doc didn't say anything. Tom asked him if he knew who Tom was. Doc seemed confused and said nothing. At the hospital the orderly put him back in the wheelchair and Tom and I went along with him to his room. It was painted some kind of institutional fluorescent off-white and there was a small bed in there with high railings on both sides like a crib for a giant baby. The orderly sat Doc in a chair and he seemed almost catatonic. In the room there was not a picture, a letter, a scrap of clothing, an indication of any kind as to the deep, richly embroidered fabric that had constituted the vibrant, colorful mantle of Doc's life.

I had stood by the door as my father directed a soft, one-sided conversation toward the anthropological remains of his old friend. Tom finally came over to the door, said good-bye one more time, and we both watched Doc stare mutely at something neither of us was yet able to see. As we started to leave, Doc, still staring into space, spoke the last words we would ever hear him say: "I love you, Tom."

★

"C'mon," said the judge, grabbing my arm. "Something's goin' on in the other wing."

Indeed there was.

Nurses, orderlies, and sheriff's deputies were scurrying around like mice under a birdfeeder at midnight. The focus of the activity, we soon discovered, was a room belonging to one Gertrude McLane. The same name on the scrap of paper I'd shown to Judge Knox. The recipient of a dozen yellow roses.

They were there, all right. In a vase in a corner. Gert was there, too. All we could see, however, was a stick leg and a birdlike hand reaching out from the middle of an electronically operated bed that someone had raised both ends of until they'd met cruelly at the top.

The judge and I stared in mute horror until we heard a familiar voice and wheeled around. It was the grim and imposing form of Sheriff Frances Kaiser.

"You're late for the slumber party," she said.

25

★ ★ ★ ★ ★

"Many years ago, around a campfire much like this one," Uncle Tom was saying, "a tribe of Indians were gathered. It was the custom of the tribe at the end of the day for the old chief to stand up by the fire and anyone with any problems or questions could ask his advice at that time. He was a wise old man and had been chief for many, many years."

Not unlike the apocryphal Indian tribe, the children were gathered on their blankets under the stars listening to Uncle Tom. Not unlike the chief, he was a wise old man and Uncle Tom had been Uncle Tom for many, many years. Casting my mind back upon everything that had happened since I dropped off the laundry that morning, I had a rather ennui-driven realization that Kinky had also been Kinky for many, many years. Willie Nelson had once told me that the thing he was really best at was "getting into trouble and getting out of it." Maybe I was only good at the first part.

"But some of the young bucks thought the chief was getting too old," Uncle Tom continued. "They wanted to show him up in front of the whole tribe. So they talked it over that day and finally one of them said, 'Look, I've got a plan. I'll go out and find a small bird that fits inside my closed palm. Tonight at the campfire I'll ask the chief if the bird is alive or dead. If he says it's alive, I'll squeeze my hand quickly and open it and show everyone that it's dead. If he says it's dead, I'll just open my hand and the bird will fly away. Either way, in front of the whole tribe, the old chief will look like a fool.' "

I was feeling kind of like a fool myself. After running into the sheriff at the rest home and witnessing several of Gert McLane's fragile extremities poking out of that bear trap of a hospital bed, we'd spent the rest of the afternoon in the sheriff's office listening to her lecture us like schoolchildren. It was her case, her jurisdiction, and she would do whatever it takes to keep us from meddling. Whatever it takes, she'd said. It wasn't going to take too much, I thought. I was about half ready to hop on a plane for New York, where nobody gave a damn what anybody did. What was stopping me? What, indeed.

I looked around at the rapt circle of little faces all watching Uncle Tom. Even the counselors and the older kids who'd no doubt heard this story many times were listening intently. Hell, so was I.

"That night," Uncle Tom was saying, "after the meal and the ceremonies and the stories and the dancing were over, the old chief stood up in front of the tribe and asked if anyone had any questions or anything to say. The young buck stood up in the back and came forward into the firelight holding out a closed fist. He said, 'O great chief, I have a question to ask of you. I'm holding in my hand a small bird. The question I ask you, O great and wise chief, is simply this: Is the bird in my hand living or is it dead?'

"Well, the old chief realized at once what the young buck was trying to do. He was attempting to show him up in front of the whole tribe, because whichever way the chief answered the question he would be made to appear foolish. The chief thought for a moment. Then he looked at the young man and said, 'You've come to me with a question. You say you hold in your hand a small bird and you ask is the bird living or is it dead?' "

Every child was listening and watching as Uncle Tom lifted his arm dramatically toward the sky, palm upward in a closed fist, and intoned the final words of the old chief:

" 'The answer to your question is: That, my son, depends on you.' "

Later that night, after the bell had rung for lights out, Tom, Sambo, and I were having a snack in the kitchen of the lodge. I was drinking coffee and eating a sweet roll, Tom was drinking milk and reading his newspaper, and he and Sambo were sharing a great many sweet rolls. This was a ritual with the two of them, and watching it almost gave you the sense that all was right with the world.

"No doubt about it," I said. "The sheriff means business this time. She can get a court order. She can have me arrested. She can make things a real nightmare for me if I stay on the case."

"And what does Pat Knox say about this?"

"She's part of the problem. There's the big sheriff with her hands on her hips standing in the doorway watching me leave her office and sitting there behind her is the little judge winking at me. I'm caught between two women and I'm not hosin' either one of them."

"That's a first," said Tom, as he gave Sam another sweet roll.

"Even worse," I said, "is if I hang around here, lead two-hour nature hikes up Echo Hill to the crystal beds, become active in the garden club, sing songs around the campfire, and, as a result, more people die. There's certain leads, weird hunches I'm working on that the sheriff would never follow up even if I could explain them to her. It takes a not quite normal mind to solve a case like this."

"Sounds like they need you, my boy," said Tom jovially.

"Of course they do. They just don't know it. And I don't know whether it's worth risking my health, my happiness, and my personal freedom, such as they are."

"That, my son, depends on you," said Tom, and he turned back to the sports page of the *Austin American-Statesman*.

"Is there an echo on this ranch? All I need now is a moral dilemma. Hell, I didn't get where I am letting others tell me what to do and what not to do. I've walked my own road. I've worked hard. I'm the laundry man! I'm the hummingbird man!"

Tom put down his newspaper.

"*I'm* the hummingbird man," he said, and he gave another sweet roll to Sambo.

26

★ ★ ★ ★ ★

It is not usually considered normal for a grown man to look forward each night to sleeping with a cat. But the early hours of the laundryman job and the additional stress of investigating the handiwork of a particularly talented serial killer were wearing me out. I was dimly aware that Pam Stoner, in her faded, perfectly fitting, sinuously crotched cutoffs, was staying up in the Crafts Corral to watch the kiln. I had all I could handle cuddling up with the cat and counting yellow roses. I had decided long before the campfire embers were cold that I was never going to squeeze my fist and kill the small bird. I was always going to open my hand and let it fly away. In a strange way I knew that what happened with this case did depend on me.

If you ever have a choice between humble and cocky, go with cocky. There's always time to be humble later, once you've been proven horrendously, irrevocably wrong. By then, of course, it's too late to be cocky.

"It may seem arrogant," I said to the cat, "but if I don't get to the bottom of this—find out why somebody's croaking these old ladies—I doubt if anybody ever will. Is that terribly immodest?"

The cat, who was by nature, of course, wholly self-absorbed, did not seem to particularly care.

"As Golda Meir once remarked: 'Don't act so humble—you're not that great.' "

The cat affected no reaction whatsoever to this statement. The politics and culture of the Middle East had never held much interest for her. Her idea of a fascinating place was probably Sardinia.

Around eleven-thirty I poured a shot of Jameson's down my neck a little too quickly and almost needed a Heimlich maneuver. Hell of a way to go. Hank Williams, Gandhi, and the cat all hanging around watching you choke to death. By about the time Cinderella met the guy with the shoe fetish I'd managed to recover enough to put on my sarong and go to bed. But I didn't sleep.

I was thinking of a recurring motif in this case. Something besides the obvious—the yellow roses, the victims being old ladies all of an age. It was a little detail, I was sure—unimportant, inconsequential, just barely pricking my consciousness. Just a feeling I'd seen or heard something several times that I should've paid more attention to.

I thought of a conversation I'd had with Tom a few weeks back about baseball. I'd asked him who, in the history of baseball, was the all-time rbi leader by the all-star break.

"Jimmy Foxx," he'd said.

"Wrong."

"Not Jimmy Foxx?"

"Not Jimmy Foxx. Not Jimmie Rodgers. Not Jimi Hendrix."

"Who's Jimi Hendrix?"

"Played in the Negro leagues. You give up? Okay, I'll tell you. Hank Greenberg, in 1935—103 rbi's at the all-star break and they didn't even pick him for the all-star team."

We both shook our heads in dismay.

"That's right," said Tom, "I remember. The manager was Mickey Cochran, a vicious anti-Semite."

"It's still a pretty good piece of trivia."

Tom looked at me for a moment, then seemed to stare off into the long ago.

"There *is* no trivia," he said.

As I played the conversation back, in the wide open spaces between my ears I realized that Tom's last sentence was a great truth. There is no trivia. The principle applied to life, to love, to baseball, to murder investigations. Even to trivia.

I was thinking these trivial thoughts and jimmying with the door of dreamland when I heard a loud clanging sound echoing in the darkness somewhere near my head. The cat and I both leaped sideways. To my relief, it was only someone knocking on the door of the trailer. A trailer, particularly an older model like mine that isn't ever going anywhere again, has a submarine-like metallic skin that can turn a normal knock in the darkness into almost a psychedelic auditory experience.

I opened the door of the green trailer and saw two green eyes staring into my own. It had to be either a nuclear jackrabbit or else Pam Stoner had decided to take a break from watching ceramic leaf ashtrays glowing in the kiln.

"Come in," I said. "You scared the shit out of me."

"I have that effect on some men," she said.

I walked over to the bottle of Jameson's on the little counter beside the sink and poured out two stiff shots. Pam lifted her glass in a toast.

"Here's to the big private dick," she said. "I hope you find out who's killing all the little old ladies."

"How did you hear about that?"

"Oh, you know what they say. The ranch is a rumor factory. A girl hears things."

"And all the time I thought I was successfully disguised as the lonely laundryman of life."

"Don't worry. All your secrets will be safe with me. And I'll bet you've got a bunch."

We clinked glasses, killed the shots, and I felt my hand move softly through Pam's boyish hair and down her woman's body. She had that rare ability some women possess of looking stunning and sensual even by bug-light. I kissed her once gently. Then longer and harder until her lips took on the familiar feel of the well-worked webbing of a kid's first baseball glove.

"I'll tell you a secret," I said.

"You already have."

27

★ ★ ★ ★ ★

When Chuck Berry made his one and only trip to Disneyland and saw all the inflated figures of Disney characters there to greet him at the entrance, his first words reportedly were: "Fuck you, Mickey Mouse." That was pretty much the way I felt about the sheriff and her minions, one of which, I noticed, was waiting the next morning in a plain-wrapped squad car as Dusty and I flew over the cattle guard and drifted down Highway 16 toward Kerrville. A guy with a big head and a big cowboy hat began following us at a respectable distance.

"We seem to have picked up a tail," I said.

"Your washer fluid is low," said Dusty.

"After last night," I said, somewhat confidentially, "your washer fluid would be low, too."

Dusty coughed politely. The sheriff's deputy stayed there like a flyspeck in the rearview mirror. It was as good a place as any for a sheriff's deputy. The dance cards they'd been dealt in life were rarely very full. Not that I myself lead a bustling, industrious existence; I just had better things to do and places to be than a flyspeck on somebody's rearview. So I decided to proceed with the investigation until I was forcibly restrained from pursuing the truth. And pursuing the truth, I knew from experience, was almost as difficult and dangerous as pursuing happiness. I also had observed in my travels that the two pursuits were somewhat star-crossed, for just when you finally found one of them you always seemed to have mysteriously misplaced the other.

I pulled Dusty into the parking lot of the little flower shop by the Veterans Cemetery, with the flyspeck still in the rearview and a sense of foreboding clouding the horizon. The guy had just opened the place and was moving pots of flowers around hither and thither when I walked in the door. I did not receive the reception I'd been expecting. The guy, who before had seemed almost ready to give me ether on a piece of Kleenex, now, quite inexplicably, seemed thrilled to see me.

"Kinkster!" he shouted. "Let me introduce myself. Boyd Elder's the name. Why didn't you tell me you were the Kinkster?"

"I'm not the Kinkster," I said, stalling for time to figure out what the hell was going on. "I'm a Kinky impersonator."

Boyd Elder laughed. He was friendlier but he still had that dangerous, high-pitched, redneck laugh going for him. Laughter's a signature that's hard to forge.

"I've been readin' all about you," he said. "Right here in the *Kerrville Mountain Sun.*" He waved the newspaper before my disbelieving eyes.

"Yep," said Elder, "that's a right interesting case you're workin' on. How many little old ladies been killed? Is it five or six?"

"Let me see that."

Elder forked over the paper and I skimmed the front-page story. It was today's paper, the byline was J. Tom Graham, and just about everything, including my involvement in the case, was pretty much public knowledge now. This would change the river for sure. Kick the investigation into overdrive. And, much worse, possibly create a dangerous sea change in the killer's mind, not to mention spreading sheer terror amongst the geriatric multitudes in the Hill Country. On the other hand, the case was not exactly galloping to a conclusion. Maybe if we got everything out in the open, the killer would die of exposure.

"Anything I can do," Boyd Elder was saying, "I'll be happy to help. Boy, can you imagine that. Comin' all the way down here from New York to tackle this murder case here in Kerrville. Once a Texan, always a Texan. Right, Kinkster? I *can* call you Kinkster?"

Boyd Elder laughed again. Same laugh. He was probably going to die laughing. If he wasn't careful I was going to speed the plow a bit and strangle him with my own hands.

"You want to help," I said, "here's how you can do it. Those flowers you sent to Gert McLane last week. The lady at the old folks' home on Water Street. Could you find out who ordered them?"

"They were ordered by phone. Let me check out the credit card stub. Be right back."

He went into his office and I could hear him riffling through files and drawers and generally being busy as a little bee helping the big private dick who'd come all the way from New York just to solve the case. That hadn't been, of course, my reason for coming down to Texas, but I had to admit, it looked good in print. I scanned the story again and wondered what the hell was going to happen now. Any one of a million things. The killer could take a sabbatical till things cooled off. He could become more brazen. Try to contact the newspaper, the sheriff, or even the Kinkster. He could thrive in the media attention and increase his killing pace. Anything was possible. All bets were off now.

"Here we go," Elder was hollering. "Good bookkeeping always pays off." I took the little slip of paper from the florist.

The name on the slip was V. Finnegan. There was also a phone number and credit card number. Elder very obligingly let me take the credit card stub and the newspaper. We swapped phone numbers and hobbies and I told him I'd be in touch if I thought of anything else.

"You've been a big help," I said. "This may bring us a lot closer to identifying him."

"I'm not so sure," said Elder.

"Why not," I said, putting the stub in my pocket and lighting up a cigar.

"*Cherchez la femme*," he said, in an accent hideous enough to make any self-respecting frog hop for the nearest puddle. But I wasn't a frog and I wasn't a prince. I just wanted the story to be over.

"Spit it, Boyd," I said. "What the hell are you talking about?"

"The caller," he said, "was a woman."

Elder didn't laugh.

Neither did I.

Chapter

28

★ ★ ★ ★ ★

I popped into Pampell's to have a cup of coffee, settle my nerves, and see if Jimmie Rodgers' ghost was still hanging around the old opera house. After the third vaguely familiar person asked me how the case was going, I got a little nervous in the service and bugged out for the dugout. I drove Dusty past the ranch cutoff and over to Earl Buckelew's place. I needed to get away from people for a while and Earl's was perfect for that. Just Earl and his six-toed black tomcat. Neither of them asked too many hard questions. I knew the sheriff would not be happy with the *Mountain Sun* story. I doubted if my father would be overly pleased with it either, since it clearly was a giant step toward the destruction of the separation between ranch and state. Not only was I prominently mentioned in the piece, but so was Echo Hill. It wasn't precisely best foot forward to base your murder investigation out of a summer camp for children.

"So now," said Earl Buckelew, gesturing with his cane toward his own copy of the *Mountain Sun*, "*he* knows who *you* are and *you* don't know who *he* is."

"I don't even know for sure if he's a he," I said. "It was a woman who ordered the flowers sent to the last victim. Also, it'd take a pretty fair seamstress to sew somebody's lips together. You don't sew, do you?"

"I don't sew, I don't chew, and I don't play with girls that do."

I showed Earl the credit card stub with the phone number. "Looks like a local number, doesn't it?"

"That'd be Bandera."

"Mind if I make a call or two on your phone?"

"Long's you don't call Australia," he said. I noticed he was wearing his "I Climbed Ayers Rock" cap. In 1985, about six months after my mother died, Earl, Tom, McGovern, and I—the Four Horsemen of the Apocalypse—had visited Piers Akerman and his family in the land down under. Our adventures, no doubt, will be chronicled on another occasion, but it is not entirely inconsequential to note that Earl enjoyed himself immensely on the trip and developed somewhat of a clinical recall whenever Australia is mentioned. I was determined to head him off before he got out the photo albums.

"Let's see what happens when I dial the number of this V. Finnegan lady who ordered the flowers."

"It'll be disconnected," said Earl, leaning back in his grandfather's old green rocking chair.

"We don't know that," I said, getting up and walking over to Earl's old phone on the wall. "Here we go—555-8826. . . . It's been disconnected. How could you be so sure of that?"

"No killer that's worth a shit is gonna give you his phone number that easily."

"You'd make a good detective."

"Beginner's luck," said Earl, and he winked. Very few people know how to wink and fewer still know when to wink, but Earl Buckelew knew both along with a lot of other human talents and that's just one little reason why I've known him forever and it still seems like the wink of an eye.

"Okay, so it's disconnected. Let's try the credit card company. It's a 1-800 number."

"Sure you're not callin' New Zealand?"

"More likely New Jersey."

When McGovern and I left Australia, Earl and Tom had stayed on and traveled to the outback and to New Zealand. Earl, having once been a champion sheepshearer, loved New Zealand, where there are more sheep than people. I've long suspected there may be more sheep than people in America, too, these days. It's just harder to gather the statistics or, for that matter, the wool, because it's harder to tell them apart. Having left Tom and Earl to their own adventures, McGovern and I had traversed to Tahiti, where we encountered a highly disproportionate number of transvestites and honeymooners, and from where McGovern set sail for Rarotonga and I returned for a gig I couldn't get out of in the States, thereby becoming the first white man to ever fly from Australia to the Jewish Community Center in Houston, Texas.

I dialed the 1-800 number and listened while some automated nerd ran down the whole menu of buttons to push if you wanted to hang yourself from a shower rod and finally got around to telling you what to do if you had a rotary phone. Earl, of course, had a rotary phone. For Earl it was still a rotary world and maybe, considering the frantic, mindless, unhappy nature of modern times, it was the best of all possible worlds. The recorded voice told me to wait.

I waited.

Then a real live, bright, chirpy, young woman's voice came on the line and said: "This is Debbie Ahasuerus. How can I help you?"

"I'm just checking a recent billing on my card. I don't recall making the purchase." I gave her the account number on the stub.

Debbie Ahasuerus had the information right at her fingertips. I hardly had time to light my cigar.

"The card member's responsibility for this account has been terminated," she said. "And we have a note. Our security department's been cooperating with the Kerr County Sheriff's Office on this matter. We'll just continue to leave the account open. Is that all right?" It looked like the sheriff was indeed on the case.

I took a rather unsteady puff on the cigar. "Yes, that's fine."

"And the corporation extends its condolences, sir, on the passing of your wife, Virginia."

I mumbled a few appreciative words to Debbie Ahasuerus and hung up the phone. There was a ringing in my head as I turned to Earl, who was rocking in his old chair and staring thoughtfully off into the middle distance at something that probably had happened before I was born. Then the sudden reminder occurred to me, accompanied by a slight shiver, that the solution to this mystery might very well lie in something that had happened before I was born. Back when the rotary phone was the coming thing.

"Earl, you got a phone book around here?"

"Over on the table somewhere there's an old one."

"That'd be perfect."

I sorted through barbecue, cookies, donuts, and cakes that his kids and admirers had brought him. With gout and high blood pressure, Earl's doctors had decided that he shouldn't eat anything and Earl had decided the hell with them. The phone book was there, all right. About the size of a comic book. The year was 1989. Close enough for line dancing.

Bandera made Kerrville look like a big town, so it wasn't hard to find Virginia Finnegan. There weren't any other Finnegans or any other Virginias, so that was that. However improbable it was, it had to be.

"Earl," I said, "you remember that old lady in Bandera who drowned in the bathtub about six months ago?"

"I recollect I do."

"Well, here's something else to recollect. She just called the florist and ordered a dozen roses."

I didn't know what the hell was going on but I sure as hell was determined to find out. Why would a woman who drowned in her bathtub be ordering roses six months later? She shouldn't even have any business ordering a rubber duck. I knew, of course, that it hadn't been Virginia Finnegan, the first apparent victim, who'd placed the order. It was no doubt somebody who had taken her credit card and, very probably, her life.

I knew from limited personal experience, and from long late-night talks with Rambam, that some of the biggest souvenir hounds in the world were serial killers. They almost never dispatched a victim without retaining something for the wall, the album, the hidden drawer, or the dusty old hope chest up in the attic. The keepsake might be a credit card, driver's license, photograph, article of clothing, finger, eyeball, or forget-me-not swath of pubic hair. If you stopped to think about it, the serial killer and the trophy hunter had a surprisingly similar mindset. There was little difference in the game they played—only in the game they hunted.

I was a hunter, too, I reflected, as I sat at my little desk in the green trailer and listened as the shouts and laughter of the children lightly segued into a chorus of cicadas and a lonely whippoorwill calling long distance to its mate. I was a hunter who tracked the wide open spaces between the ears of a madman, just barely within shouting distance of reality. Me and my shadow of death strollin' down the avenue. No season. No limit. No regulations. God was the game warden. If there was a God. And if it was a game.

The cat and I were alone, but there was a certain intensity in the air. I'd brewed a large pot of coffee that lent an ambience vaguely reminiscent of some long-ago Bobby Kennedy campaign headquarters. Along the inner walls of the trailer where the little watermelon children once frolicked, Pentagon-like profiles of the seven victims were now pinned. But the portraits were pitifully incomplete. Patterns were not plentiful.

Virginia Finnegan was a square dancer. Myrtle Beach belonged to the Daughters of the Republic of Texas. Amaryllis Davis played bridge. Prudence South was a hyperactive Republican. Octavia Willoughby was a member of the garden club. Beatrice Parks, Pat Knox's recently discovered victim, had been a Red Cross volunteer once upon a time. And Gert McLane, who'd died in bed not quite as peacefully as she might've desired, didn't even have a hobby as far as I could tell. What a shame, I thought, to go through life and not even be able to tell St. Peter: "I was an adult stamp collector."

They'd all died on their birthdays. But their lives seemed to have almost nothing in common. At least nothing I could hang my cowboy hat on. In the days ahead many trips to the

Butt-Holdsworth would be in order. Many phone calls to Pat Knox, J. Tom Graham, the Boyd Elders, the Debbie Ahasueruses of the world. Many cups of coffee.

Hank and his old pal Gandhi looked on with a glint of encouragement or possibly only curiosity in their eyes as clusters of worshipful daddy longlegs gently undulated upon the placid, glassy waters of their respective high rodeo drag.

Uncle Tom would not be happy with this trailer as a spiritual command center for a murder investigation. Sheriff Kaiser wouldn't be rapturous, either. That made three of us, for I was hardly a happy camper myself. I was homesick for somewhere I'd never been. For life to be complete. For death to be kind. Or at least for it to be aware that it was cutting into my cocktail hour.

I'd left room on the wall for profiles of future victims. There'd be more where these came from. Death, I suspected, wasn't going to sleep. Death didn't know it yet, but neither was I.

30

★ ★ ★ ★ ★

"What a damned circus," Pat Knox said as she sipped a cup of coffee and smoked a cigarette at her small desk in her small office. The door was locked. The secretary wasn't letting through any calls. It was just the two of us and a banana tree that was twice as tall as the little judge and looked about the way I felt. It made sense that if you stayed up pursuing investigative obituary half the night, in the morning you were going to feel half dead. The other half didn't feel too good, either.

"Seven victims," said the judge, as she poured half a cup of luke joe into the pot containing the banana tree. "Damn," she added. "I'm not supposed to do that. It's not good for it."

"Who told you coffee's bad for banana trees?"

She didn't seem to hear me. Just got up and poured herself a fresh cup, killed the cigarette, lit another, and sat back down at her desk.

"Seven victims," she said. It was getting to be a mantra. "You'd think there'd be an overall, coordinated campaign of some kind, tests for semen, DNA—anything—after seven victims."

"The sheriff doesn't care if it's twelve maids a-milkin'," I said. "She's going to run the investigation at her own pace—"

"And scare the livin' bejesus out of every old lady within a hundred miles of here? There's so much we're in the dark about. I hear the sheriff's brought in some psychiatrist from Waco."

"They *have* psychiatrists in Waco?"

"What I hear, they think the killer's someone who hated his mother."

"Where would they get that idea?"

"It's just so damn frustrating not to know what's going on. Not to be able to help. I know it's crazy but I still have the feeling these are sex crimes as well as—"

"Hold the weddin', Judge. I can tell you right now that the last one wasn't. The McLane woman died when she was sandwiched by the mechanical bed. If the guy'd raped her he'd have to have been Houdini just to get his pee-pee out in time."

The judge killed another cigarette and stared at the banana tree. "You do bring a certain sophistication to the case," she said.

I belched the words: "Thank you, Judge."

She continued her communion with the banana tree and didn't crack a smile. There wasn't a lot to smile about. Someone in the Hill Country was getting away with murder, and damned if it seemed there was anything the two of us could do to stop him. To make matters worse we were confined to a very limited, clandestine role in the whole rancid scenario, like two hoboes plotting together under a trembling trestle as the freight train of law enforcement rumbled by overhead on the way to nowhere.

I walked over to the coffee pot, filled my cup again, and studied the large map of the Hill Country that occupied almost the whole wall of the judge's office. Little pins, dates, names of victims, all reminded me a bit of my own crime setup inside the green trailer. It was kind of poignant to see how Pat had set this up in her lonely little office, ostracized from the official investigation, no one to share ideas with but the banana tree, almost like a kid with a lemonade stand in a bad location.

"Look," I said, "we may not have access to the experts, we don't have much manpower, we don't have state-of-the-art police procedural mechanisms—"

"What the hell *do* we have?" said the judge.

"We have two people who smoke and drink a lot of coffee and have a lot of accumulated miles along the rusty lifelines of human nature. You were the first person to realize that these deaths weren't accidental, that they were related and methodically planned. I've had some passing experience butting heads with the NYPD, and while the races haven't always been all that pleasant my track record ain't too bad. I think the two of us can solve this thing."

The judge stood up to her full half-banana-tree height and raised her coffee mug.

I raised my cup as well.

"L' Chaim," I said.

"What's that mean?" said the judge.

"Objects may be closer than they appear in the mirror."

Ten cups of coffee and three trips to the little private investigator's room later, Pat Knox and I had burrowed our way
through the victims' profiles once again, coming up with no
consistent element other than the obvious: old widows getting
themselves croaked on their seventy-sixth birthday. The judge
hadn't left her desk except to get more coffee. Now we were
both standing before the giant map on the wall.

"I find it amazing," said the judge, "that having lived full
lives during a rich, colorful era in Texas history, by the time
they die all anyone can recall is that Myrtle was in the Daughters of the Republic of Texas and Octavia belonged to the local garden club."

"I find it amazing," I said, "that a person of your size could
have such a remarkable bladder."

"Thank you very much," the judge said humorlessly. We
both looked at the map some more.

"This is not the pattern," I said, "of your garden-variety serial killer. Your Ted Bundy or your Henry Lee Lucas."

KINKY FRIEDMAN

"He ain't *my* Henry Lee Lucas," said the judge.

"The point is, Your Honor, a serial killer selects victims from a general population when, for whatever reason, they turn him on, so to speak. He has a little problem with blood lust. The killings almost always tend to escalate in terms of savagery and in their coming closer on the heels of one another. The downtime when the killer rests or goes out to play miniature golf usually becomes less and less as his murderous pace picks up. That's when he gets a little careless. That's when he usually gets caught. But I don't see any evidence of that here."

"You're saying he's working on a preselected population."

"Correct. A special population."

"You don't think the shrink could be right? Maybe he's a drifter, a stranger who's been knocking off old ladies in other places before he came here because he hates his mother?"

"It's unlikely. Let's say he's a monstro-wig that just blew in from Uvula, Texas, where he's been whacking little old ladies. Assume he's got some way of knowing when birthdates of geriatric widows roll around. There's lots and lots of seventy-six-year-old women who *aren't* getting croaked around here. Everywhere you go there's a little old lady right in front of you driving four miles an hour. Which brings us back to the twisted green fuse that's driving this whole case. *How* does he pick his victims? If we can determine that we might figure out *why.*"

"He's a local boy, I just know it. I don't care what crap the shrink is tellin' the sheriff, this ain't no cry for help. He don't care if he gets press or not. I think he'd just as soon as not. And he sure as hell doesn't want to get caught."

"I agree," I said. "But if he's media-shy he's going to have some problems. The wire services and *Unsolved Mysteries* can't be far away. There's people in L.A. and New York right now who're probably working on screenplays and book deals for him. He's going to need an agent."

"He's gonna need more than that if I get my hands on him. If I just knew where to look."

"There's only one place you *can* start looking for a killer you can't find and you can't understand."

"Where's that?" said the judge.

"Inside yourself," I said.

★

A fat man in a plain-wrapped squad car stopped picking his nose as I slithered out of the justice of the peace's office. His eyes followed me as I crossed Main Street against the light and almost got T-boned by a cement mixer. I'd always thought it would be kind of sad for a cosmopolitan figure like myself to get his ass run over in Kerrville, Texas, but I suppose there were worse fates. Agamemnon comes to mind.

I popped into the Smokehouse to buy a box of Hoyo de Monterrey Rothschilds from Clint and JoLyn. Before Clint and JoLyn bought the place, Bill and Betty Hardin had sold me cigars at the Smokehouse. Before that I'd bought most of my cigars in New York. Two hundred years from now when archaeologists are searching for the tomb of Shithead the First I'll probably be comfortably ensconced in hell buying cigars from Lenny Bruce and Gertrude Stein.

"Tell us all about the case," said JoLyn as I walked in the

door. "There's a big story in today's paper that if you and the sheriff and the local authorities can't find the killer they may call in the Texas Rangers."

"They always get their man," I said, as my eyes roved past the titles of almost every used paperback in the world except *Steal This Book*.

"That ain't the Texas Rangers," said Clint, puffing on his pipe. "That's the Canadian Mounties."

"I knew somebody always got their man," I said. "Of course, it'd be a little silly callin' in the Canadian Mounties."

"So it's true," said JoLyn, "that he's already killed seven people and there's no clues."

"Actually, there are some clues. At the scene of each crime the killer's left a used paperback."

"Kinky!" said JoLyn.

"He's kiddin', honey," said Clint.

Then she leaned over the counter confidentially. "Tell me," JoLyn said, "what's it like to work on a big murder case like this with the sheriff?"

"It's a thrill a minute," I said. "We have a very caring, sharing relationship."

I entered the walk-in humidor before JoLyn could ask me any hard questions. The door closed behind me and left me all alone in a peaceful, rarefied atmosphere with thousands of quiescent cigars in neat little rows like children in a Rumanian orphanage waiting for their moment in the sun.

Whenever I walked into a humidor I always remembered the time many years ago in L.A. at a big tobacco store in some big shopping mall. Kent Perkins and Jim Ryder were with me as we found ourselves inside one of the largest, lushest humidors we'd ever seen. Just being inside the humidor felt like you were making love in a tropical jungle. I've done both in my lifetime—been in humidors and made love in jungles—and which is the more satisfying experience is a hard call to make without instant replay. But the humidor seems to shut out reality to a greater degree—allows you to cast your mind back to some Tennessee Williams childhood more vivid and colorful than the one you've no doubt already repressed. And there's the added advantage of the humidor that you are very unlikely to suddenly be rear-ended by a large hippopotamus.

At any rate, Kent and Jim and I were in this humidor when for no particular reason I emitted one of the loudest, longest, most enormous farts of my adult life, much to the dismay of my other two humidoreans. At just the same moment, the owner of the store, who of course had no way of hearing or gauging the phenomenon, came striding purposefully over to the humidor, possibly to help us with cigar selection. Kent and Jim and I were all laughing by this time. As Dylan Ferrero once observed: "Seventy-five percent of all men find farting humorous and zero percent of all women."

"*God damn*," said Perkins, "that was a world-class bell ringer."

"It sure wasn't one of them whiny, high-pitched, little Brenda Lee farts," said Jim supportively.

At that precise moment the owner of the place walked into the humidor. One of the high-water marks of my life was watching his eager-to-please, unctuous, American smile fade as the noxious vapor wafted across the humidor signaling

him that something was terribly wrong. His entire demeanor
and total countenance became that of a person with the soul
of a North Korean businessman . . .

A strong hand on my shoulder quickly brought me back
from this blast from the past. I spun around in the little room
and saw a vaguely familiar face. The kind that takes you a lifetime to place and then you wish you hadn't.

It was Boyd Elder.

"Didn't mean to startle you, Kinkster," he said.

"Never sneak up on a veteran."

"Oh, were you in Nam, too?"

"No," I said, taking a box of cigars down from the top
shelf. "Gallipoli."

"You know the other day," said Elder, "when you were in
the store I was so excited reading about your being on the
murder case that I forgot to tell you something. You said to
keep in touch if I thought of anything. It might be nothing. It
might be important."

"Spit it," I said. The humidor was becoming mildly claus-
trophobic.

"There's a guy I know, sort of a strange survivalist type.
Lives out in the country like a hermit."

"So far it could be me," I said.

Elder laughed. Then he got serious.

"Not quite," he said. "This is one of those kind of guys that
somehow manage to fall through the cracks, as they say. No
family. No close contacts. No driver's license. No Social Security. No phone. Gets in touch when absolutely necessary
through ham radio."

"Wish more people were like him."

"No, you don't. He was in Vietnam, a special forces commando. Tells stories about coming back from the jungle and taking live canaries out of their cages and eating them for lunch. Half the weaponry used in the war has somehow come into his ownership. Took a piece of shrapnel in the head and has some motor control as well as emotional problems."

"Sounds like a nice chap to sit down to tea with."

"He lives out Harper Road." At this juncture, Elder took out a notepad and drew a rough map for me showing how to get to the survivalist's place. I took out a cigar, went through the pre-ignition procedures, and wondered if I was going to survive this conversation.

"He's also a beekeeper."

"No law against that," I said. "Sherlock Holmes was a beekeeper in his later years."

Boyd Elder looked at me and I could tell that just describing the guy was starting to give him the heebie-jeebies.

"He also raises roses," said Elder.

I lit the cigar, rotating it slowly in my right hand, carefully keeping the tip just above the level of the flame.

The guy's name was Willis Hoover. It was entirely possible that going after him would result in a futile, somewhat dangerous wild goose chase, but at this point every lead had to be followed up. I'd never had a rendezvous with a half-crazed, gun-loving survivalist at his isolated command center before. I wasn't even sure what to wear. Possibly an ancient suit of body armor might be appropriate. Bring an attack duck with me. But there had to be a first time for everything, I thought. Just as long as the first time didn't turn out to be the last thing you ever did.

So after waking up to "Wipe-Out" and feeding the cat and slurping three cups of hot black coffee I called Pat Knox's office.

"Hello, dollface," she said when she got on the line.

"That's Mr. Dollface to you," I said. "Look, Judge, I'm going out to follow up a tip from Boyd Elder, the guy at the flower shop. I'm going to see this weird survivalist type who lives way out Harper Road."

"I'll come with you."

"Well, I don't think that'd really be best foot forward. This will be kind of a male bonding experience. The guy is close to being a feral man. Probably hates all women, children, and green plants. Except roses. Loves roses. *Raises* roses, in fact."

"Except for the roses bit, the guy sounds a lot like you."

"Yeah. He could practically be my gay computer date. But I'd like you to find out what you can about him. Name's Willis Hoover. Does that ring a bell?"

"Not even a cuckoo."

"Well, check him out if you can. And if I don't call you at home by ten o'clock tonight, send out the search party."

"You sure you want to do this alone?"

"Your Honor, the guy doesn't like groups and he doesn't like anybody even faintly on the periphery of the law. He and I should get along perfectly."

"He may also be the break we've been waiting for. Now if you run into trouble, you call."

"Sure thing," I said. "And when he sews my lips shut I'll send up smoke signals with my cigar and hum a few bars of 911."

★

There was no way to call Willis Hoover and I had a distinct feeling that he was the kind of person who did not like surprises. So I got my security shotgun out of the back of the closet and loaded it up with eight shells. I made sure the safety was on. Didn't want to blow my head off before I got out of the cattle guard. The gun wasn't going to be much of a threat to a guy like Hoover. He probably had a walk-in closet full of AK Fuckhead Specials or whatever happened to be the most lethal illegal weapon of the moment.

I leaned the shotgun up against the wall, poured another cup of coffee, and lit up a cigar. I sat down in the sunlit doorway of the trailer and sipped the coffee, smoked the cigar, and reflected upon the subject of loners in this world. There've been some very good loners down through the ages. Henry David Thoreau, Emily Dickinson, Johnny Appleseed, the woman who worked with gorillas in Africa whatever the hell her name was, even Benny Hill in the last years of his life after they cancelled his television show. These people all knew that the majority is always wrong, and even if it isn't, who gives a damn anyway. They knew that *within* is where it's at, and if nothing's happening within it doesn't really matter if your co-dependent wife throws a black-tie surprise birthday party for you and hundreds of well-wishers show up who would just as soon wish you'd fallen down a well.

I liked loners. The downside, of course, was that every serial killer who'd ever lived had also been a loner. Well, you can't have everything. People just tend to drive you crazy after a while. That's why penthouses, nunneries, sailboats, islands, and jail cells do such a booming business. And trailers.

I took a solitary puff on the cigar, looked up through the blue haze, and realized that I wasn't alone. Three little girls, Pia, Briana, and Tiffany, were standing under the cedar tree in front of the green trailer. I stared at them like a man waking up from a dream. They returned my gaze curiously. At last, they spoke.

"Okay," said Pia. "Pick a number between one and ten but it can't be one or ten."

"Can't be one or ten," I said. Since I was going out soon to very likely get my balls blown off, another unlucky number to choose would be two.

I picked seven and kept it to myself.

"Don't tell us the number," said Briana.

"Wouldn't think of it."

"Now," said Tiffany, "multiply your number by nine. Okay?"

"Okay," I said. "I've got it." I now had sixty-three, and while I liked these three little girls I wished they had not chosen this particular time to visit my trailer and browbeat me with a mathematical puzzle I did not as yet enjoy.

"Add the two digits together," said Pia. "All right?"

Adding the two digits together produced nine and also produced a slight degree of tedium on my part. I stoically smoked the cigar.

"Have you added them together?" shouted Bri.

"Yes!" I shouted back.

"Okay," said Pia. "Now subtract five."

"Okay. I've got it." The number was four and, congenitally unable to keep a secret of any kind, I was having difficulty retaining this life-or-death information unto myself. At least, I felt, the exercise must be nearing its conclusion.

I was wrong.

"Now," said Bri, jumping up and down, "find what letter of the alphabet goes with your number."

I stared at her in mute pain.

"You know," said Tiffany. "One is A. Two is B. Three is C. Four is D . . . "

"All right," I said grimly. "I've got it." The corresponding letter was "D," and if this didn't cease very quickly I was going to clear my throat with a ceiling fan.

I went back inside the trailer and poured another cup of coffee to try to stave off a headache that seemed to have come on rather suddenly. When I came back the girls were still there and all three of them appeared to be highly agitato.

"Is that it?" I said. "Can I tell you the letter?"

"No! No!" they shouted. "Don't tell us the letter!"

"Fine," I said dismissively. "That was really a fun little game."

"Okay," said Pia. "Now think of a *country* that begins with your letter."

"You're kidding."

"No," said Bri happily, "we're not."

"Okay," I said, "I've got a country."

"Don't tell us what it is," warned Tiffany.

"All I'm going to tell you is I'm about ready to hang myself from the shower rod." It was beyond my imagination that this puzzle could continue for so long and be so incredibly complex. It frazzled my remaining brain cells. But at least I had the country.

"Okay," said Pia. "Now think of an *animal* that begins with the *last letter* of the country."

I stared disbelievingly into some morbid middle distance halfway between Echo Hill and the Monkey's Paw in New York. This game, if it was a game, was truly interminable.

"Think of an animal that begins with the last letter of the

country!" said Bri as if she were speaking to a two-year-old.

"Okay," I said grudgingly, "I've *got* it."

"Now," said Tiffany, "think of a color that *begins* with the *last letter* of your animal." I told myself this was the last time I'd ever have even a passing relationship with a child. Even if I lived to be a kindly old man I would never speak to a child again.

"Do you have the color?" demanded Bri.

"I've *got* it," I said.

The girls looked at me in a state of high delight. I looked back at them in a state of total ennui, which soon transformed itself to total dismay.

"We didn't know they had orange kangaroos in Denmark," they all shouted together.

I was stunned.

"How did you do it?" I said.

"A girl can't reveal all her secrets," said Bri. "What's the gun for?"

The girls all craned their necks and looked into the trailer at the shotgun leaning against the far wall. I turned and gazed at it, too. It made an ugly little still-life painting.

"I may go on a little hunting trip later this evening."

"You're not going to kill anything?" said Pia with a look of disgust.

"Of course not," I said. "It's strictly for self-defense."

"Self-defense against what?" asked Tiffany.

"Orange kangaroos in Denmark," I said. "Now go back to your activities."

Chapter

33

★ ★ ★ ★ ★

Dusty and I wound our way up Harper Road with the shotgun in the trunk and the late afternoon sun hanging low like a stage prop in a summer-stock sky. I thought of an incident Dylan Ferrero had mentioned to me that had once occurred on Harper Road. Dylan had been driving by several years ago and saw what he thought was some kind of petting zoo by the side of the road. A number of wild animals were in caged enclosures and a group of people with young children were walking around looking at the animals, petting, and feeding them. Dylan stopped because he remembered seeing a large black water buffalo like the kind he and I plowed rice patties with in Peace Corps training in Borneo. Dylan communed with the buffalo for a while and then left just as a long black limousine was pulling up.

Dylan had a few errands to run and when he came back down Harper Road about a half hour later he noticed that the water buffalo was gone. He stopped the car and looked around, and sure enough, no water buffalo. He and several stray children walked around to the back of the enclosures and there in the dust was the cleanly severed head of the water buffalo. The kids were in tears and Dylan was stunned as he asked the guy who ran the "menagerie" what in the hell was going on. The guy explained the buffalo had been sold to a customer in the limousine who only wanted the head for his trophy collection.

"Why would he just want his head?" one little girl tearfully asked Dylan.

Dylan didn't have anything cued up in the old answer machine for that one. Indeed, it remains an adult riddle to this day.

I rarely enjoy telling or hearing animal death stories and this one doesn't shed any light or gloom on Harper Road particularly, nor does it tell us anything much about animals. The only reason I include the story here is because it tells us something about ourselves.

"Why would he just want his head?" I asked Dusty as I followed Boyd Elder's crude little map to what I expected would be Willis Hoover's crude little place.

"Prompt service is required," said Dusty, as we turned left and headed up a steep, rocky incline.

I checked the rearview and saw nothing but road behind me. It was ironic that the one time the sheriff's department had decided not to shadow me might be the occasion on which I needed them the most. Ah well, as my old friend Slim used to say: "You's born alone, you dies alone, you best as well get used to it." Parts one and two of Slim's credo, of course, were usually more easily accomplished than part three.

We flew across three cattle guards down a lonely road with

nothing to break our line of vision but scrub live oak and sinister cloud-shadows that seemed to palpably waver in the heat that enclosed us like a giant microwave. The only signs of life were the dark, peripheral flutterings of the buzzards as they watched from dead trees along the roadside. This definitely didn't look like the way to grandmother's house.

"Men have been known to freeze to death on the equator," I said to Dusty. "Especially when their washer fluid is low."

Dusty shuddered violently.

We pulled off the gravel road near an old ramshackle log cabin that looked like the Beverly Hillbillies might've lived there before they moved. I cut the engine and carefully stepped out of the car to suss out the situation.

"Don't forget your keys," said Dusty.

"I didn't forget them," I said. "We may be departing rather quickly."

Nothing appeared to be moving around the vicinity of the cabin, so I walked a little closer. The cabin was atop a small rise, a good vantage point for Hoover to have if waves of Mexicans, communists, Martians, or pointy-headed intellectuals ever tried to capture his somewhat dilapidated command post. There was a deathly quiet about the place, broken only by what sounded like Dizzy Gillespie playing a rather large, mean kazoo. The noise seemed to be emanating from somewhere in the back of the cabin.

I crept quietly along the little path that led up the small hill and discarded several possible cover identities as I went. Jehovah's Witness didn't really fit the bill. Sneeze-guard inspector for salad bars didn't feel right either. AmWay representative had a reasonable ring to it.

Then I saw the flowers.

They literally took your breath away. Beds and beds of roses of all colors and sizes, in that lonely, godforsaken place looking for all the world as beautiful as the butterflies etched by children into the unforgiving walls of Auschwitz. Could a hand with such a remarkable green thumb have so much blood upon it? Could the same mind that created this beauty be capable of the premeditated murders of seven human beings?

With the roses to my right and the cabin to my left I headed toward the Dizzy Gillespie area across the pathway of worn-down flagstones. It was hard to believe that I could very well be tracking a serial killer right into his lair. But that was part of the problem. A serial killer doesn't usually look like a serial killer. In fact, the serial killer rarely resembles what we think of as a criminal or a monster. He does not radiate evil. More likely, he comes off in the manner of the genial host at the weekend suburban barbecue or that friendly, outgoing, nice-looking delivery man. Why would he just want his head?

The kazoo-playing was getting louder. So was the intermittent pounding of my heart. This was either a ridiculous wild goose chase or, very possibly, I was about to get goosed by God. Suddenly, the feather in my cowboy hat was flying through the air with the cowboy hat still attached. I was, unfortunately, still attached to the cowboy hat. The roses were swirling like those in a painting by a minor French Impressionist. I was caught in some kind of old-fashioned snare trap swinging upside down like a human pendulum about six feet off the ground. The kazoo music, which I'd by this time deduced to be bees, had a nice little Doppler effect going for it each time I swung back and forth. Or it just might've been the blood rushing to my head.

This was it, I thought. I either should've been more considerate of others or less considerate of others during my lifetime. I definitely should've been something, because I was going to end up as a humorous little news story: MAN STUNG 7,000 TIMES BY BEES. Of course, the tabloid play would probably be quite a bit more sizable. That depended, naturally, on a number of other factors. How much weight Delta Burke gained this week. How much Magic Johnson lost. What particular peccadillo Elvis Presley, Marilyn Monroe, Teddy Kennedy, or the Virgin Mary had gotten involved in recently. Any little thing like that could blow me right out of the tub. I could almost hear the editor of the *Globe* shouting: "Hold the back pages!"

It might make a good B movie, no pun intended, but it was always a shame when the peculiar mode of someone's death held more interest for people than the tone and timbre of the person's life. Greater men than myself had fallen victim to this unpleasant little foible of human nature. I wasn't certain that Nelson Rockefeller was a greater man than myself, but it'd certainly happened to him. Bigger in death than in life. God gave him a wife named Happy. So what does he go and do? Checks out while he's hosing his secretary. That didn't make Happy very happy.

It didn't make me very happy, either, when I saw coming toward me a little man with a head that looked like a toadstool. His gloved hands were held strangely in front of him and seemed to be shaking like a crab. He took off some kind of pith helmet with a long bee screen attached that had previously hidden the upper part of his body. Now he just looked like a kindly, congenial, chuckling, everyday serial killer.

"Glad you came by," he said. "Why don't you hang around for a while?"

Then he disappeared around the corner of the little cabin.

Chapter

34

★ ★ ★ ★ ★

Now there was a problem. Hanging six feet off the ground upside down with one foot in a noose was just the kind of activity that could be hazardous to your health. You could learn a little more than you wished to about the birds and the bees, the birds in this case being the buzzards which were already slightly tightening their little circles overhead to get a better look at the catch of the day. Buzzards will eat anything that formerly moved and now doesn't. To them everything tastes a little bit like dead armadillo.

The prospect of a huge swarm of abandoned honeybees, moderately irritated by the sudden departure of their master and coming upon me like something out of Gullible's Travels, was a most unpleasant alternative to the buzzard scenario. An equally tedious potentiality was that the animal kingdom would leave me alone and the beekeeper would return, possibly mistaking me for a large bee. And Willis Hoover's congeniality worried me. He certainly seemed friendly enough to be a serial killer.

My cowboy hat fell off and drifted and scalloped to the ground like an awkward mutant black snowflake. I continued to hang by one foot. With enormous effort I managed to reach into the right front pocket of my jeans and extract my Chinese version of the Swiss Army knife, which had undoubtedly been made by Chinese prison labor because I'd bought it for three dollars on Canal Street. I'd bought several of them at the time, all from a large Negro with purple pantyhose on his head who was talking to an imaginary childhood friend. Guy like that you don't want to christian down too hard.

I'd given one of the knives to my dad and I remembered him telling me: "My father once gave me a knife like this and now my son has." Funny what you think about when you have a little time on your hands.

From my ankle to my head the pain was increasing, and if I never had before I now truly empathized with every animal in the wild that was ever trapped by the clever, cruel hand of man. I opened the knife and made a few passes at the rope, but the knife was too dull and the rope was too strong. I shouted for a while, but the only answer was the buzzing of the bees and the ringing in my ears. Hoover was probably inside the cabin tapping his foot to an eight-track of The Captain and Toenail and gaily sprinkling a little Equal on his serial.

I felt like crying. I remembered I hadn't cried at my mother's funeral and when the rabbi shook my hand he'd said: "I see it hasn't hit you yet." I hadn't answered him then. But the truth was it'd hit me a long time ago. Now it was hitting me again. All life ever does is hit you when you least expect it, and all you can ever do is laugh or cry whenever the hell you feel like it. As they say, "Anything worth cryin' can be smiled."

For some reason I also thought of Patrick O'Malley, who was a homeless person back in the early seventies in Nashville when people used to call them bums. For some reason "bum" sounds more dignified even now than "homeless person." Patrick was an aristocratic freak and proud to be a bum, and he hung around our little house off Music Row with Billy Swan and Willie Fong Young and Dan Beck and myself in the days when we were getting the old Texas Jewboy band together. Patrick, who's no doubt hustling handouts in heaven about now, had any number of memorable credos. One of the best was as follows: "If there's two things I can't stand it's a shitty baby and a cryin' man."

That was probably why I hadn't cried at my mother's funeral.

The bees, the beekeeper, and the buzzards were all beginning to cut into my cocktail hour, so I made one desperate, somewhat herculean effort to grab the rope with one hand and slash it with the other. I felt the knife tearing into the strands of the rope and I felt the combined power of millions of Chinese criminals, many of them no doubt political prisoners, pulling and sawing and ripping the twisted fabric of a spiritually outdated society.

The rope gave.

Bees buzzed.

Flowers flashed by.

Then everything went black. Black as the cemetery that night when I'd met the judge. And I knew, just before the curtain came down, that the solution to these murders lay in the Garden of Memories.

I woke up some time later to what sounded and felt like a racehorse pissing on a flat rock inside my head. I opened my eyes slowly in the darkness and made out the rough form of a strange man carrying a flashlight and a water bucket. He poured the water on my head and shined the flashlight in my eyes. I was glad he wasn't the beekeeper. I was glad just to be at the party at all.

"Goddamnit!" he said. "You spooked his ass!" I had no idea what he was talking about but it was oddly comforting hearing a human voice.

"Sherlock Holmes was a beekeeper," I said.

"Fuck a bunch of beekeepers," he said. "Now we gotta go after his ass, and he knows these hills like a ringtail coon."

It dawned on me that this man was a sheriff's deputy and that Willis Hoover, possibly through my intrusion, had headed for the hills.

"Is the sheriff here?" I said, rubbing my ankle.

"Sheriff was here she'd run your ass right into the sneezer. She ain't, but I am."

"So it's just us fellas," I said.

"Shit," he said, and spat disgustedly on the ground dangerously near where my cowboy hat had come to rest.

In the distance I could hear more cars driving up, voices shouting in the night, dogs barking. Here and there, searchlights began to penetrate the darkness. They looked like little lighthouses on an ocean of dust.

"This here beekeeper's our number one suspect in the killin's."

"The killin's?"

"Them little ol' ladies. Now, what's your name, buddy? Sheriff'll probably be wantin' to talk to you."

I got up gingerly and limped over to pick up my hat. Then I took out my wallet and fished out my card and handed it over to the deputy. He shined his flashlight on it and studied it for a long while like it was a dead sea scroll.

The card read: "Kinky Friedman is allowed to walk on the grounds unattended. If found elsewhere, contact: Echo Hill Ranch, Medina, Texas, 78055." And it gave my phone number.

"I *know* the sheriff's gonna want to talk to you," he said. "I didn't know who you were at first but now I do. Sheriff told us about you."

"I'm the legendary what's-his-name," I said.

"Well, you can get goin' and stay gone," said the deputy.

"That's good," I said. "I was getting tired of holding on line two."

I put on my hat and limped away. Then I climbed into Dusty and got the hell out of there.

"A door is ajar," said Dusty, as we drove away.

★

The ranch was quiet and peaceful as we splashed across the causeway and pulled into the parking area very slowly with headlights off. At Echo Hill it's always considered best to let sleeping ranchers lie. It was about a quarter past Cinderella time when I parked Dusty in front of the green trailer, went in and poured a generous shot of Jameson's, went back outside and sat in an old wooden chair, and leaned up against the trailer. One of the most comforting things to know in life is that even if you feel everyone in the world's let you down you can always lean on a trailer.

I sipped the shot and relaxed and watched the horses grazing in the parking area. Farther over on the flat I could see deer and jackrabbits and I could hear a group of counselors talking and laughing in the dining hall. On the archery range a horse was chewing the straw out from under one of the targets, another case of exactly what Uncle Tom didn't want to happen.

The little line of bunkhouses set against the base of Echo Hill itself all were in stillness with their porch lights glowing yellow like a village of island people, which in a sense, I suppose, we were. The scene looked like it'd been painted by Gauguin on tequila. I took another swallow of Jameson's and heard the dull thudding noise of the cat jumping from the roof

of the trailer and landing on top of the air conditioner. The air
conditioner had been dysfunctional long before most modern
mental landscapers had heard of the word. Like most modern
mental landscapers it blew only hot air. From the top of the
air conditioner the cat's next move was to wait until I'd gone
to sleep, then jump through the open window and land on my
testicles. I could hardly wait.

I was getting up to walk to the Jameson bottle when the
phone rang. I collared it quickly.

"Start talkin'."

"So you made it safe and sound." It was the judge.

"Well, let's not go that far. I've been hangin' upside down
like a large grouper for most of the afternoon but I am alive
and able to answer your phone call at this time."

"Well, I found something out about Willis Hoover."

"So did I. Never sneak up on a veteran."

"He's done some prison time. Do you know what for?"

"Insider trading?"

"Try rape. And the victim, I understand, was an older
woman."

★   ★   ★   176   ★   ★   ★

36

★ ★ ★ ★ ★

It wasn't a particularly pleasant feeling to know that Willis Hoover was roaming the hills possibly in a half-crazed predatory state and that I had done my little bit to put him wherever the hell he was geographically and emotionally. Not that I spent a lot of time blaming myself. He was a big beekeeper. Besides, with every law enforcement nerd in the Texas Hill Country scouring the hills for his ass, how long could he hold out? He couldn't remain on the run forever. Even a survivalist has to survive.

In the days following Hoover's flying the coop I hung around the ranch, although not by one foot, and tried to work out a few little matters in my still somewhat bruised head. Had the sheriff's department tailed me out to Hoover's place without my knowing it? Had Boyd Elder or someone else given the sheriff the same tip that I'd received in the Smokehouse? Or had the sheriff checked out Hoover's criminal record, at least twenty years old apparently, and got onto him by herself? It was very much a Sherlock Holmes–Inspector LeStrade relationship I enjoyed, so to speak, with the sheriff. As Emily Dickinson wrote: "Though we are each unknown to ourself / and each other, / 'tis not what well conferred it, / the dying soldier asks / it is only the water." That was Emily's convoluted and beautiful way of saying it didn't matter who actually solved this case just as long as somebody caught the bastard.

The judge, J. Tom Graham, and myself began telephonically to pursue a concentrated campaign aimed at isolating the nature of the "special population" that apparently made up the victims of this peculiar and very particular monster. Again and again, as Inspector Maigret might have done, we delved into the pasts of the victims. Needless to say, we did not find the tie that binds one life to live to search for tomorrow. The sands of time had done their job well, it seemed, for the further back we looked the less there was to see. And there appeared to be nothing, beyond the superficial similarities that everyone already knew, that might engender any special qualities exclusive to our special population.

"Most of the women were Republicans, of course," J. Tom had told me recently.

"Hell," I'd said, "*all* seventy-six-year-old women in the Texas Hill Country are probably Republicans. If I was a seventy-six-year-old constipated, humorless woman living in the Texas Hill Country I'd most likely be a Republican, too."

J. Tom had laughed. "Maybe the killer's a Democrat," he'd said.

"I'd opt for libertarian."

"Anyway, I just wanted you to know I'm feeding all the data on the seven victims into the computer. We may soon have some interesting results."

"I'm not optimistic. Computers understand the human mind about as well as the Japanese understand baseball. They play by all the rules, but when a player makes an error on a Japanese team—even if he's a star player—the manager immediately benches him. That shows that even with their zealous efforts to imitate our culture like a monkey in a zoo, the Japanese have never truly understood the spirit of baseball."

J. Tom had apparently nodded out briefly during my Japanese-computer analogy, but when he came to, he jumped right back on where he'd left off.

"It's somewhat arbitrary," he'd said before he hung up, "but I'm considering four to be a significant number in a universe of seven."

"A universe of seven," I'd repeated to the cat.

★

The conversation had occurred a few days ago and I still hadn't heard back from J. Tom on any computer results. It would be galling to have the case solved by a computer, I thought, but " 'tis not what well conferred it, / the dying soldier asks / it is only the water." I was beginning to understand Emily Dickinson's mind, and that was also cause for some worry on my part. On the other hand, if you could truly understand Emily Dickinson you just might be able to figure out where a guy like Willis Hoover was coming from.

37

★ ★ ★ ★ ★

It was one of those hot, almost-mythical Texas summer nights where you drop off to sleep not knowing if you're a man or a child and you wake up in the morning half-wishing you were an angel.

I never got to the angel part.

I was deep in what seemed to be a rather pleasant routine dream about my brother Roger the psychologist walking around naked with my cat on top of his head. Both parties, though it would've been quite out of character under normal circumstances, seemed to be enjoying themselves enormously. Man and cat appeared to be smiling beatifically and this, of course, caused me and Hank Williams to smile crooked little semi-beatific smiles ourselves and even produced a mischievous little serial-killer-type smirk upon the otherwise passive countenance of Gandhi, almost as if he'd broken one of his famous fasts with a hearty bite of beansprout vindaloo.

I was just considering getting some lip chap balm for

Gandhi when a loud metallic sound began reverberating through the dank night air, sending all the smiles undulating slightly like large lobsters in the death-row tanks of some trendy restaurant far from the sea. Emanating occasionally from the sumptuous dinner tables could be heard the ugly sounds of rich people laughing.

Suddenly the trailer door was opening and in walked a fifteen-year-old junior counselor named Danny Carl, who was taller than the Holy Ghost returning and appeared to be about twice as agitato.

"Kinkster!" he shouted. "Come quick! The Mavericks are on an overnight at Big Foot and there's a huge swarm of killer bees buzzing anyone who moves!"

Danny Carl was the ranch belching champion, the perennial winner of the Counselors Night belching contest, having only been defeated once at the hands, or rather, mouth, of Katy Sternberg in a much-disputed, somewhat bitter belchoff during first session the previous summer. Danny could belch the entire alphabet in one sustained belch—a sure crowd pleaser.

All championship belchers in the history of the ranch had belching regimens they followed religiously. Katy Sternberg favored Coca-Cola to enhance her efforts and, as I recall, competed one year with a sustained belch of "Jump! Shake your booty! Jump! Jump! Shake your booty!"

Eddie Wolff, a daunting competitor, insisted upon a diet of raisin bran and Seven-Up before all major contests. Danny Carl believed exclusively in pork rinds. I myself, in my salad days before becoming a CBE (Championship Belcher Emeritus), had always sworn by the Chocolate Soldier, a hard-to-find carbonated drink that long ago had fallen out of favor, not to mention flavor.

In last summer's contest, the one in which Danny had only gotten as far as "U" in the alphabet, there had been a nice, engaging repartee amongst the competitors, all conveyed, of course, in sustained belches. "I'm better than you," belched Danny, to which Eddie belched back, "But I'm bigger." Katy responded with "I want to win!" to which Eddie replied "That was good for a girl."

Katy went on to win the championship with a terrific, gut-wrenching rendering of the phrase: "I Am Woman, Hear Me Roar." Wayne the wrangler, who was also involved but was never considered to be a really serious competitor, finished the contest by vomiting on the gray truck. Wayne's regimen, at this writing, is not known to me.

But Danny Carl wasn't belching now; he was scared. His demeanor did not appear to relax measurably as he saw me walk across to the little closet and extract the large 12-gauge riot gun.

"You're not going to get many of them with *that*," he said, looking at me as if I were walking around with the cat on top of my head.

"I'm not my brother's beekeeper," I said in a somewhat sphinxlike manner as I walked out the door and climbed into Dusty. Danny got into the passenger seat along with Sam, who didn't like the shotgun but was a car whore as long as he could sit in the front seat. There was not a lot of room in the passenger seat even for one normal-sized American and Danny's large adolescent body combined with an excited Sambo created yet another situation in which, when Danny closed his door not quite completely, Dusty found it necessary to remark: "A door is ajar."

Moments later, flying on adrenaline and moonlight, we splashed across Big Foot Wallace Creek and arrived at the campsite. I killed the engine and when the dust had settled we saw that the place looked deserted. I gingerly got out of the car and listened for any sound, human or otherwise. It was the otherwise I was worried about.

As our eyes adjusted to the semidark terrain we could see a group of figures by some trees down by the creek. No sign or sound of the bees. We walked down the small rise and Floyd, the nature-study counselor, came out to meet us.

"No sign of the bees for about ten minutes now," he said, staring pointedly at the shotgun I was cradling. "What in the hell did you bring *that* for?"

I pulled Floyd aside for a moment, waved to the kids with a confidence I didn't feel, and scanned the dark horizon for any sign of man or bee. There was none. Probably it was just a coincidence that I hadn't seen a swarm of bees in the Hill Country for many years and now I'd had close encounters with two swarms in the same week. Most likely these bees, wherever the hell they were, had never even heard of Willis Hoover. But it was a chance I couldn't take. What if they'd followed him over here? What if they'd followed *me* over here? In my head the whole situation was taking on the proportions of a Shakespearian tragedy. To bee or not to bee.

"What *did* you bring the shotgun for?" Floyd was asking me again.

In terse tones I explained to Floyd about my recent adventures with Willis Hoover. I told him Hoover was a fugitive and possible serial killer and I asked him if there was any way the bees could've accompanied him here to the ranch.

"The only way," said Floyd, "would be if he took the queen with him. If he did that, the rest of the swarm would very likely follow. Of course, he'd have to be pretty crazy to do that."

"All beekeepers are crazy," I said. "Not to mention serial killers."

"Well, if that's what you're worried about, it's very doubtful that this is the same swarm. It's probably just a hive that one of the kids bumped into in the dark. Bees don't usually display much activity once it's dark. I think you can put the shotgun away. You might take out a cigar and puff on it. They're not really all that fond of smoke."

There was something in Floyd's light, knowledgeable approach and something in his eyes that reminded me strongly of his father, a man who'd known more about the out-of-doors than anyone I'd ever met, and I found this comforting. I walked over to Dusty, put the shotgun in the trunk, and went down to the bank of the river where Floyd and the kids all were.

"Why'd you bring the shotgun?" asked one of the boys.

"To blow Ernest Hemingway's head off," I said.

I took out a cigar and lit it up to buy time and calm my nerves. Floyd winked at me just like his dad would've done. I'd taken about three puffs when a loud buzzing blur that sounded like the Mighty Eighth came roaring through the air just over my left shoulder.

"Everybody in the creek!" shouted Floyd.

As the bees began swarming in a slow, low, dangerous circle, twelve kids, two counselors, Floyd, and myself all hit the
creek with one mighty splash. Sambo did not like to swim but
I noticed him crawling under Dusty for protection. Jewish
shepherds are pretty smart.

"As long as they don't start stinging anybody we're okay,"
said Floyd. "If someone gets stung a number of times the
mind of the swarm may take over. Then the bees may go into
an attack mode."

"What happens then?" I asked, with only my mouth and
one ear above the surface of the water.

"We're fucked," said Floyd.

"So what happened next?" asked Marcie some time later, as she rocked in Aunt Joan's favorite old rocking chair in the white trailer.

"Well, the bees circled for a while like a giant black lariat and then some kind of group consciousness thing happened like Floyd was telling me about. The mind of the swarm told them they'd scared the shit out of us enough and it was time to go home to the hive."

"Then what did you do?"

"We all ran like hell out of there. Floyd and Danny took the boys back to the bunk to change out of their wet clothes, and they were all last seen heading down Armadillo Canyon with Bucky to a new campsite at Three Rivers."

"I'm surprised you didn't even get a bee in your bonnet."

"I am, too. The Lord protects middle-aged over-the-hill country singers."

"He didn't do too good a job with Johnny Horton," said Marcie. Johnny Horton had recorded such hits as "North to

Alaska" and "Sink the Bismarck" before dying in a head-on collision near the Texas–Louisiana border back when today's country singers were still spermatozoa swimming around in little black cowboy hats.

"When do you think you'll solve this murder case?"

"Probably on a cold day in Jerusalem. I have a nagging feeling there's something we're all missing but I can't for the life of me figure out what it is. It's something to do with the victims. I just feel that those seven old ladies were kind of like the swarm mentality of the bees. I've got no evidence to prove it, but I'd swear that they knew each other."

"If they did, it could've been a very long time ago."

"That's what's so difficult and so spooky about this case. If something happened so long ago, what kind of person would care after all that time? Who would still hold that sort of grudge? And why wait all those years?"

"What you've got to do," said Marcie, "is operate like the jewfish. I've got his picture here in this old fish book from the fifties."

I glanced at the picture of the large, scaly, bloated-looking creature.

"Attractive," I said.

"Okay," said Marcie, "here's what it says: 'With the cunning of its race, the jewfish—' "

"It doesn't say that!"

"It sure as hell does. 'With the cunning of its race, the jewfish sucks up everything around it and then spits out what it can't digest.' "

"Jesus Christ. Talk about the 'warlike Apache.' The fuckin' jewfish. It's kind of like Sherlock Holmes, who sucked up everything around him and spit out the impossible, thereby leaving him—improbable as it might've seemed—with the truth."

"Then you ought to be able to solve this case with what you already know. You've been investigating the damn thing for half the summer. Now go ahead and figure it out. Let the jewfish be your guide."

I went back to the green trailer and got out my Big Chief tablet and a fresh cigar. With the cat sitting under the desk lamp watching, I reviewed my early notes on the victims like a demon in the night. What social interaction could've occurred long ago and had such impact that the victims might've still known each other later in life, as I suspected? Garden club? Bridge club? Senior square dancers? All were fairly geriatric pastimes.

Okay, starting with Amaryllis Davis. Lifelong member of the Daughters of the Republic of Texas. What did I know about the DRT? Nothing except that they were a group of old ladies who protected and kept up the Alamo as a state shrine. I'd seen them there. Tour guides. Caretakers. Lots of plaques. Plaques. Where'd I seen a plaque recently? Ah, yes. The Garden of Memories Cemetery.

Octavia. The one we thought was the killer's fifth victim until we saw the six yellow roses on her grave. But that wasn't the point. The point was that we'd been thinking "garden club" when it came to Octavia. Garden club and her lips having been sewn together. We hadn't computed that little stand with the plaque on it beside her grave that proclaimed her membership in the DRT. That made two—that we knew about—in a universe of six which quickly became a universe of seven.

But what about the dream that old lady had about her sister? I was frantically flipping pages in the Big Chief tablet when there came a knock on my trailer door.

"Come in," I said, still flipping pages.

Pam Stoner walked in with her light blue shorts and dark green eyes. "I'm taking a short break from watching the kiln," she said. "There's a lot of pieces in there tonight and if it gets too hot something might explode."

"I know what you mean," I said. She sat down on the bed and the cat immediately jumped in her lap, which was kind of a blessing because I had to concentrate tonight and it might be distracting watching her cross her legs. She was a world-class leg-crosser.

"Pam," I said, "ever heard of the Daughters of the Republic of Texas?"

"No," she said. "They're not big in Oklahoma. What do they do?"

"I don't know. They sort of protect the Alamo."

"They're a little late for that, aren't they?"

"Well, you know, they keep it from becoming a parking lot or a Bennigan's."

Pam thought about it for a moment, then glanced around briefly. "Another couple years they might consider protecting your trailer," she said with a smile.

I smiled back at those big green eyes.

"Pam," I said, "do you know what a cotillion is?"

"Sure. It's a formal ball."

"You mean it's not a long-necked lizard from West Texas?"

"Your Daughters of the Republic of Texas probably held cotillions when they weren't busy protecting the Alamo. Those blue-blooded society groups always had their debutantes and coming-out parties and cotillions and secret ceremonies and stuff like that. They usually trace their family trees back to the Bible, study their coats of arms, keep a lot of secrets among themselves that nobody else really wants to know—"

"*I* want to know!"

"They *damn* sure aren't going to tell *you*."

"No, they're probably not."

But they'd already told me something. At least Violet Crabb had. Her sister Myrtle, the second murder victim, had come to her in a dream wearing a white formal dress and speaking the word "cotillion." That, if I didn't miss my guess, was three in a universe of seven. Three of the victims had probably at some time been involved with the DRT. As the cat leaped off Pam Stoner's lovely lap, I made a leap in my mind. I'd now bet anything that at one time *all* of the victims had been in the DRT. The DRT was how they'd known each other. The DRT held the secret to why they were murdered.

"In the morning I'm going to the Alamo," I announced.

"Congratulations," said Pam. "In the morning I'm teaching handicrafts. Can I ask you something?" She crossed her legs.

"Anything," I said.

"Do you have any regrets about this summer? I mean, other than not solving this case you're investigating?"

"Of course I have regrets. Everybody has regrets. Ringo

Starr, the drummer for the Beatles, said his main regret was that he never got to see the Beatles. My main regret this summer is that I've been so involved with this murder investigation and you've been so busy guarding the kiln that the two of us haven't had any real chance to be together much."

Pam laughed, somewhat ruefully, I thought, and got up and went to the door.

"I have a regret, too," she said, stepping out into the moonlight and heading back toward the Crafts Corral.

I walked over and stood in the doorway and watched the moonbeams bouncing lightly off her beautiful backside.

"What's your regret?" I said.

She stopped and turned around and stood there for a moment. Her tennis shoes and Echo Hill T-shirt as impeccably white and pure as the snow on a postcard mountain. Her blue shorts as challenging and defiant as a battle flag in the heat of sacred war. Her eyes as proud and deep and mischievous as Ireland.

"I haven't seen a long-necked lizard yet," she said. "I understand they only come out at night."

In most criminal investigations things will slog along interminably like slow dancers in a rather humid dream until suddenly everything seems to be coming unwrapped at once. So it was that, instead of heading off to San Antonio the first thing that morning to pursue the DRT connection at the Alamo, I found myself picking up the blower and listening very foggily to the stentorian voice of Sheriff Frances Kaiser.

"Well, we brought him in last night," she said.

I wasn't sure if she was talking about the Christ on the cross or the duck in the hailstorm, but it worked for me.

"Who'd you bring in?" I said, as I fumbled with the many moving parts of the percolator.

"Willis Hoover," she said. "The beekeeper that buzzed off when you made your little unannounced visit to him."

"Sheriff—"

"Well, I'm callin' a meetin' this mornin'. Just you, Judge Knox, and myself in my office at nine o'clock. Can you make it?"

I looked at my watch. It was 8:07. "I'll be there," I said.

"Good," said the sheriff. "Now that we've caught this bird, we want to be sure we can clean him and cook him." She hung up while I was still holding the blower.

"I'll be there," I repeated to the cat.

★

I arrived at the courthouse punctually and had almost got in the front door before some officious bureaucrat wagged her finger at me for smoking in the hallway. When a bureaucrat's officious it's rarely auspicious, I thought. But the sheriff proved me wrong. The meeting was brief, harmonious, and almost what is referred to in political circles as cordial. All three of us felt that Hoover was our man. None of us felt very comfortable with what we had on him, which was very damn little other than circumstantial evidence and our gut feelings.

I mentioned that I'd like to follow up on a possible DRT connection to the case, and I received affirmative head nods from both the sheriff and the judge. The judge said she was looking further into Hoover's background, and the sheriff and I expressed our approval. The sheriff said it was time for all of us to work together and do whatever it takes to nail this monster and put the fears of the community to rest. We all heartily agreed. In fact, the only thing about the meeting that was even mildly disconcerting was how much in agreement we all were and how well we seemed to get along with each other. It felt good but it didn't quite feel right.

At the end of the little meeting the sheriff said there was something she wanted to show the two of us. She led us down the hall and down another corridor and stopped outside a small courtroom.

"There he is," she said.

The little judge and I peered around the body of the sheriff and saw Willis Hoover standing in the dock. A small man who seemed nervous and somewhat overawed with the perpetual legal peregrinations he was experiencing. His hands were shaking in their cuffs and his eyes were on his shoes.

"Don't look like a serial killer, does he?" said the sheriff.

"They never do," I said.

"You ain't gonna let in the Boston Strangler," said the judge, "if he *looks* like the Boston Strangler."

"You can stitch that one on a pillow," I said.

★

A short time later Dusty and I pulled up onto I-10, set our ears back, and headed for the Alamo. It was going to be a hot day, yet I still detected a trace of residual chill from peeping in upon the human refuse that was Willis Hoover. It was even now hard to separate the little, harmless-looking man from what he had allegedly done. There must be another soul within him somewhere. Of course, he hadn't been proven guilty yet, but that might now be just a matter of time. Circumstantial evidence from all three of our investigations pointed clearly at Hoover, who had the classic profile of someone who'd fallen through the cracks of society and in that way evaded detection. He'd run from me, he'd run from the law, he'd raised yellow roses, he'd served time for raping an older woman, and, according to the sheriff, he'd refused to profess guilt or innocence. Now that I thought back to him standing in that room, I could almost see the evil radiating outward in sympathetic ripples, yet I also felt a somewhat grudging pity for the pathetic little creature.

The Alamo was still there, of course. I'd often said that if the state of Texas were ever engulfed in nuclear attack, the only two institutions left standing would be the Alamo and former Dallas Cowboys coach Tom Landry's hat. Of the two, the Alamo was the one I chose to always wear with pride.

With the morning burning off and the pigeons and tourists fluttering around, the sight of the Alamo caught my heart again as it nearly always did. It was a small, poignant, pock-marked little mission, standing blindly in the sunlight as if it might not survive the coming night. It was not full of itself, nor was it distinguished by the bigness that Texans often brag about, yet it was by any consensus our state's most cherished possession. But we did not really possess the Alamo; it possessed us, as it possessed free people the world over who saw it or read its story. The Alamo was not a Texas brag, I thought. It was just the opposite. The humble heart of Texas. One of the few shrines I'd ever attended worthy of a prayer.

On the battle-scarred door is a plaque—the DRT is very big on plaques—that reads:

> *Be silent, friend.*
> *Here heroes died*
> *To blaze a trail*
> *For other men.*

To the right of the door is another plaque. This one reads:

QUIET
NO SMOKING
GENTLEMEN REMOVE HATS
NO PICTURES
NO REFRESHMENTS

As my friend Dr. Jim Bone says: "A lot of rules for a small company."

I killed my cigar and took off my hat, rubbing my hair carefully so my head wouldn't look like a Lyle Lovett starter kit. That certainly wouldn't go over well with the Daughters.

Then I went inside.

Davy Crockett's beaded vest has always been like a Shroud of Turin for me. I stare silently at it and its hundreds of beady little eyes stare silently back at me. The vest was worn by a true American hero—a man who died not for home, for land, for country. In truth, he was just passing through. He died because he was in the right place at the wrong time. He died with a hell of a lot of dead Mexicans lying all around him like a bloody funeral wreath. He died before he ever saw a car or a computer or a video. He wasn't even a Texan. But he was everybody's kind of man. In a world bereft of heroes, Davy still stands tall.

These were roughly my thoughts when I noticed another figure standing rather tall beside me. It was one of the younger DRT women who'd become somewhat agitato about the unlit cigar that I'd unconsciously placed in my mouth.

"Don't light that," she whispered.

"Don't be silly," I whispered back. "Do I look to you like a person who'd smoke a cigar in the Alamo?"

The young woman directed a hostile gaze at me and didn't say a word.

"Do I look to you like a person who *fought* in the Alamo?" I whispered.

Moments later she was navigating me firmly back into the sunlight into the gravitational pull of an older Daughter.

"Maybe *you* can help this gentleman," she said.

"I'm Lydia McNutt," said the older lady matter-of-factly.

"I'm Phil Bender," I said. "I'm a graduate student in anthropological choreography and I'd—"

"Well, I'll be happy to tell you about the Daughters of the Republic of Texas," she said, obviously operating on some kind of clinical recall. "The organization was founded in 1903 by Clara Driscoll to honor early Texas men and women who blazed the way before statehood, to honor Texas with various holidays, and to preserve and protect the shrine of the Alamo. You do remember when it was that Texas became a state, don't you, Mr. Fender?"

"Uh, Bender. And I guess I'm not really too sure about—"

"Come, come, come! Surely you remember your high school history lessons. It was ten years after the Alamo, in 1846, that Texas became a state. To join our organization one must clearly establish through birth and death certificates that at least one ancestor lived in Texas before it became a part of the United States of America."

"My field, anthropological choreography, is a very specialized one, Mrs. McButt, and we—"

"McNutt," she said, in an oblivious, almost mindless singsong. "Lydia McNutt."

"The field is so specialized," I continued, "that we eschew all things of a political or patriotic nature—"

"You poor dears."

"Yes, well . . . and my special area of interest is 'Cotillions of the Late Thirties.' "

We'd talked for a while longer as Mrs. McNutt told me just a little more than I wished to know about the current situation of the Daughters. But, of some passing significance, she did reveal that in the early days the blueblood, upper-class traditions of the DRT were far more dominant and ingrained than they were today. And almost as an afterthought, she'd pointed across the street to the Menger Hotel, in which she believed resided an old disused ballroom furnished with archival materials. This, for once, was exactly what I wanted to happen.

I entered the historic old hotel with some trepidation, for as well as Richard King, the owner of the King Ranch, dying there and Oscar Wilde and O. Henry living there, it had been one of the two places on earth that I'd ever truly seen a ghost. I didn't know it as I walked in the door, but damned if I wasn't about to see one again.

Fortunately, my friend Ernie was manning the front desk and, it being a rather light day, he was more than happy to guide me himself to the old ballroom.

"It hasn't been used for many years except to store things," said Ernie. "The room's on the second floor in the older section—not too far from where you say you saw your ghost—"

"I *did* see that ghost," I said, as Ernie led me down an old corridor that would've felt right at home in *The Shining*.

"Oh, you'd be surprised how many of our guests have reported seeing ghosts," said Ernie.

"Yes," I said, "but how many of your ghosts have reported seeing guests?"

I remembered the night quite well, actually. It'd been about ten years ago, when Ratso was down from New York on one of his famous visits to the ranch. Ratso, Dylan, and I had gone out to see Jim and Neesie Beal's band, Ear Food, and I'd gotten to bed rather early without drinking alcoholic beverages. I was definitely not flying on eleven different herbs and spices when I saw the ghost. She looked like a gypsy girl or a Mexican dancer and she came to me in a state of semiconsciousness from which I leaped sideways rather quickly.

First I was sitting up in bed, then I was standing, and the vision of the girl still wouldn't go away. She seemed to be a beautiful young person from an earlier time. She was wearing silver earrings and a belt that resembled the latent homosexual silver concho belts that the great Bill Bell of Fredericksburg had made for Willie Nelson, myself, and other Americans who unconsciously wanted to separate their bodies into two parts. I doubt if Bill Bell had been alive when the ghost's jewelry had been made. The conchos looked like pieces of stars.

Dylan was snoring through the whole thing in the other bed and later suggested, rather insensitively, I thought, that the whole experience had probably been the result of gas. At any rate, I'd become convinced after the vision refused to disappear that Ratso, who was inhabiting the other room of our suite, had played a prank upon the Kinkster. It was the only explanation I could come up with for my having gazed into the dark eyes of this vision for over two minutes while standing on my feet fully awake thinking I was going to Jesus or Jupiter at any moment.

I had frantically followed this vision into Ratso's room, where she finally disappeared, and I was totally prepared to upbraid Ratso for running in a girl or prostitute or whoever the hell she was while I was asleep. But Ratso himself was out like a beached flounder and his outer door was chained and double-locked as was his custom in New York. After I'd awakened him, with some little effort, his suggestion was that I call Ghostbusters.

"Did you or the ghost say anything?" Ratso asked.

"The ghost didn't say anything, but at one point I did."

"What'd you say?"

"I believe it was 'Fuck me dead.' "

"Couldn't have been a real ghost," said Ratso. "It never would've missed an opportunity like that."

While I'd been reliving my earlier, otherworldly experience at the Menger, Ernie had been opening a set of massive wooden doors and now he was handing me a key.

"The light switch is on the wall," he said. "Don't touch or move anything. Lock these doors when you're through and bring the key back to me at the desk."

"Fine," I said, as I gazed into the dusty, mildly primeval darkness. "If I'm not back in about fifty years, send Richard King after me."

Ernie left and I hit the light switch.

It looked like the Make-Believe Ballroom might've looked once you'd grown up and forgotten how to pretend. Dust covered the floor, sheets and tarps covered most of the furniture, and spiderwebs covered the rows of old framed photographs on the wall. The photos could've been right out of Violet Crabb's dream. I liked old, dusty ballrooms as much as anybody but I did not share my friend McGovern's devotion to them and all they once had represented. I especially did not want to see my ghost again or hear barely audible rustlings of old silk dresses as they moved gracefully across the dance floor. I just wanted to check out a crazy little notion I had and then get the hell out of there.

I didn't know at what age young women used to "come out" in the old days. Today it was about nine. But I was betting that in those early days eighteen to twenty-one was about right for a self-respecting debutante, if that wasn't somewhat of a contradiction in terms. So it was the late 1930s that I wanted, and I just hoped to hell I was right or a lot of dust would've been stirred up for nothing. Not to mention some pretty unhappy spiders.

1936. 1937. 1938 . . . that was about right. I took out my Kinky Honor America Bandanna and wiped away the dust and cobwebs from the 1938 photograph on the wall. There were two rows of girls—ten in all. They wore formal white cotillion gowns and their hair had been coiffed in the latest fashions of the day. Their eyes looked into me as only the eyes of old photographs can. They were trying their damnedest to pull my soul into a better world that I wasn't quite ready to discover yet. Not quite ready, but almost.

Their names printed along the bottom were quite familiar to me now: Virginia, Myrtle, Amaryllis, Prudence, Nellie (evidently Pat Knox's newly discovered victim that we'd missed the first time), Octavia, and dear Gertrude (the latest victim). There were two names that I didn't know: Hattie Blocker and Dossie Tolson. I jotted the two new names down in my notebook and then I counted all the names on the photograph again.

Something was wrong here. There were ten girls but only nine names. I looked carefully at each girl, matching her with her name. The last girl in the back row was the one whose name had been deleted. So had something else. I'd only seen the phenomenon before in early revisionist Russian photographs where certain political figures had fallen from favor. Seeing it here and now in this old attic of a ballroom sent a cold, timeless, unforgiving chill of half-remembered history through my very being.

Not only was the young girl's name missing.

So was her face.

"Mule barn," said Earl Buckelew, as he habitually answered the phone.

"Earl!" I shouted from the pay phone in the lobby of the Menger Hotel.

"Kinky Dick!" he shouted back.

"Earl, I've got a problem. It involves two women—"

"That's always a problem."

"The problem is that I don't know them and I'm hoping you do." I lit a cigar in the enclosed phone booth and it soon filled up with the very pleasant aroma of good Honduran tobacco.

"Just a minute," said Earl. "Let me turn down the television." I heard the sound of Earl's cane clumping across the floor to the television, then I heard it again, quite distinctly this time, on the return trip to the phone.

"Damned A-rabs and Jews goin' at it again," he said.

"We just can't help ourselves, Earl."

"Cowboys and Indians," he said.

"Anyway, you ever heard of Hattie Blocker or Dossie Tolson?"

"I never heard of that last one, but Hattie—if that's the same damn one I remember . . . "

"How many Hatties can there be?"

"Oh, you go back a ways, you'd be surprised. There'd be a Hattie poppin' outta every rumble seat."

"This one's about seventy-six years old, Earl, and she's not likely to be poppin' out of rumble seats anymore, and I've got to find her to try to get some evidence about a man we believe has already murdered seven women."

"Yeah, she was a fine little filly."

"Well, the question is where is she now?"

"Back in the thirties I used to take her out in my ol' blue Model A roadster. It was the first car in the Hill Country to have a radio put in it, did you know that?"

"No, I didn't, Earl. But do you know where this woman is now?"

"Hell, it's been a while—I've lost touch with her—but it seems like I heard . . . if it's the same one . . . she's over at Purple Hills, that place in Bandera. Some people call 'em old folks' homes."

"Earl, one more question. This Hattie Blocker—this young girl you used to drive around in your Model A . . ."

"*Fine* young filly."

"Yes, I know. But just tell me one thing: Was she ever a debutante?"

"Not when she was with me," he said.

Dusty and I flew out of San Antonio like a Texas blue norther heading east with a vengeance. We took I-10 to the 46 cutoff, then blew through Pipe Creek on the road to Bandera. All along the way the girl with no name or face haunted me, her fearful featureless countenance rising up like a violated vision on the dim tie-dyed horizon of American history.

I'd called ahead to the Purple Hills Nursing Home and learned that Hattie Blocker was indeed a patient there. No, it would not be a problem for her godson, Oswald T. Wombat, to pay her a visit later this afternoon. I asked the nurse how Hattie's memory was and she said her short-term memory was almost nonexistent. I said that was a blessing and asked somewhat trepidatiously about her long-term memory. If Hattie was cookin' on another planet she wasn't going to be much good helping to nail Hoover.

"The old days are about all the poor dear has left," the nurse had said.

"Can she remember over fifty years ago?"

"Like it was yesterday."

"That's a blessing, too," I'd said.

Everything was a blessing, I thought. It's just that none of us knew it yet. Most people today didn't even realize that daddy'd taken the T-bird away until they tried backing out of their driveway and got skidmarks on their ass.

As I drove through the blazing streets of Bandera, the image of the young woman's body without a face began to get to me and I became somewhat garrulous with Dusty.

"I have this really spooky feeling that she's trying to tell me something," I said. "I've known a name without a face and a face without a name, but this poor child appears to be redlining in both departments. Yet I can hear her voice clear as a loudspeaker across a used car lot. 'Help me!' she's saying.

'Help me!' If we can't delve into the past and arrange this case in its accurate historical framework, Willis Hoover, even though he may be guilty as sin, is surely going to walk."

"There is a problem in the electrical system," said Dusty. "Prompt service is required."

42

★ ★ ★ ★ ★

Hattie Blocker looked like Barbara Fritchie on a bad hair day. I'd been to Barbara Fritchie's house in Frederick, Maryland. I'd been to Anne Frank's house in Amsterdam. Now I was at Hattie Blocker's house.

There's no place like home, I always say.

The reason there's no place like home is that home is not a place. It's a time in your life when maybe you thought you were happy, a time you think back to long after your three minutes are up. I didn't have to look back. I just had to look around Hattie's empty, antiseptic little room at Purple Hills. It could've easily been Doc Phelps's last little room at the state hospital in New Mexico. There was nothing here but Hattie and her memories. And Hattie wasn't talking.

Hell, I probably wouldn't've been talking either if I'd had one of those oxygen things plugged into my nose, everyone I knew was dead, and a strange-looking cowboy was sitting at my bedside acting like he was dying to light that cigar any minute.

"Hattie," I said softly.

Nothing.

"Hattie," I said, turning up my vocal mike, "I really need your help with this. I just saw a beautiful picture of you with your friends at the 1938 Cotillion Ball of the Daughters of the Republic of Texas. You looked grand."

Hattie said nothing but her eyes were shining. I pulled my chair a little closer to the bed.

"Hattie, this is very serious. I wouldn't even tell you this, but we need you to help us convict a criminal. He's already killed seven of the debutantes at the cotillion, Hattie."

I reeled off the list as if I were reading the Tibetan Book of the Dead and noticed that Hattie seemed to be trembling slightly. This was a hell of a way to make a living.

"Virginia . . . Myrtle . . . Amaryllis . . . Prudence . . . Octavia . . . Nellie . . . Gertrude . . ."

Hattie Blocker said nothing.

I got up from the chair and walked over to the little window. Hopeless. Hopeless and undeniably cruel. Of all the times in my life when I may have taken advantage of people and situations, this had to be the lowest. Terrifying an old lady who was already walking the garden path to heaven's door. It did not make me proud to be an American.

I looked back to where Hattie lay propped up on the bed. Still motionless. Eyes straight ahead. She looked like a little bundle of twigs. I gazed out the window again.

Then a little twig snapped in my head. I had to go ahead with this inquisition. It was too late to ask the Baby Jesus what other flavors you got? Dossie Tolson could be in worse shape than Hattie Blocker, if indeed she was even still alive.

KINKY FRIEDMAN

The girl with no face and no name was trying to get through but I was having trouble adjusting my set. I had to keep walking down Yesterday Street and hope I could get wherever the hell I was going before today became tomorrow and yesterday was lost forever to a country funeral, a hotel fire, or a cat pissing on a telephone number.

"Look, Hattie," I said with some excitement. "Look what's comin' up the road. It's Earl Buckelew in his blue Model A roadster. And you're sittin' right next to him. My, you look fine. And he's got that cute little rumble seat back there. Wait. I can hear his radio playin'. What's the song? Oh, I hear it now. 'Don't sit under the apple tree with anyone else but me, anyone else but me, anyone else but me . . .' "

I stood perfectly still, continued staring out the window. A moment passed, I suppose. What Hollywood screenwriters are fond of calling a beat. In truth, just another step down that garden path that all of us unconsciously tread every day of our lives. Hattie was just a little ahead of us in the line.

"She was a cute little thing," she said, in a surprisingly clear voice. "A saucy little redhead. The boys all liked her and some of the girls were jealous."

I gazed out the window and held my breath.

"I told that Octavia. I said, 'Octavia, you got a big mouth, honey. Don't you go spreadin' scandal. You could ruin that poor girl.' "

Octavia, I thought. Octavia. Oh, my fucking god. Octavia with her lips sewn together.

I waited. There was nothing for a while.

Then she said, "Don't remember her last name anymore.

★　★　★　**210**　★　★　★

The little redhead. But her first name was Susannah. Like 'O Susannah, don't you cry for me.' "

"Try hard, Hattie," I said. "Can you remember Susannah's last name?"

She was trying but I could see that it was useless.

"I want to sleep now," she said finally.

Her face looked like a well-loved, well-worn human road map and I suspected that Robert Frost was right. She had miles to go before she slept.

"You've been very helpful, Hattie," I said. "God bless you."

I squeezed her hand and walked to the door. At the door I looked back at the old woman and the little room.

"You really looked beautiful in that Model A," I said.

Her face was still turned to the window when I left.

Chapter

43

★ ★ ★ ★ ★

Dusty was waiting for me right where I'd left her under a large Spanish oak tree in the front circular driveway of Purple Hills. I'd just climbed in and put the key in the ignition when I saw a florist's van pull up to the side entrance. Boyd Elder got out, opened the back of the van, and, moments later, entered the side entrance of the building carrying a bouquet of yellow roses.

Maybe it was something Hattie Blocker had told me or maybe it was something I'd been unconsciously worried about all along, but the noose that had seemed to be tightening nicely around Willis Hoover's neck now appeared to be whirling wildly and wickedly like a lasso out of control in the hand of a very sick cowboy. I jumped out of the car and dashed across the driveway.

"Don't forget your key," said Dusty.

The peaceful green lawns of the nursing home belied the dark thoughts fairly zimming through my brain as I scuttled across to the side entrance like a crab on cruise control. Was it possible that we all could've missed the boat so completely? Was it possible that I'd soon be staring dumbstruck at what used to be Hattie Blocker?

The side door was locked now.

I raced around again to the front of the building and my mind was racing right along with me. Of course Willis Hoover was the wrong guy. It would have been virtually impossible to have sewn Octavia's lips together with a nervous hand disorder. And if he grew yellow roses, why order them from a store? And what about Boyd Elder? Last seen owning a little flower shop. Easy access to all kinds of flowers. Last seen helping with the investigation. Pointing us in the direction of Willis Hoover. Last seen carrying yellow roses into Purple Hills. Last seen locking the goddamn door behind him.

I bolted through the main entrance and shot down the nearly deserted corridor like a runaway bowling ball past a geezer in a wheelchair wearing a Houston Oilers cap. The Oilers were having their troubles and so was I.

"Where's the fire?" he said.

I hooked a left at the far end of the hall and slowed down halfway along the side corridor. The place was all pretty quiet and peaceful, like an old library where somebody'd checked out all the books and just never brought them back. I ankled it carefully over to the vicinity of Hattie's room. I listened with dread and was mildly relieved to hear the two voices in conversation.

". . . *two* gentlemen callers in one day," Hattie was saying. I thought that was pushing it a bit.

"Who was the other one?" Elder asked.

"Now don't be jealous," she teased. Ever the ingenue.

"I'm not jealous," said Elder patiently. "What's he look like?"

"He was *very* young," she said. "Wore a big black cowboy hat. Smoked a cigar. Of course, he didn't smoke it in here, what with my oxygen and all."

I was getting a bit jealous myself that Hattie was so voluble with her second gentleman caller.

"Of course not," Elder said. "What'd he want?"

"Who?" said Hattie.

That's my girl.

"The cowboy with the cigar," said Elder helpfully.

"He wanted to know about the girls. The girls in the Cotillion Ball of 1938," she said dreamily.

"Well, isn't that something. That's why I brought you these."

"Oh, lord, how beautiful! Are they all for me?"

"They're all for you, Hattie."

"Thank you so much. You're so kind."

"Here, I'll set 'em on the table where you can see 'em."

This guy was one sick chicken.

"So nice of you to think of me."

"Oh, they're not from me, Hattie. They're from a friend of yours."

There was a brief, rather sinister silence as Hattie possibly realized she had damn few friends left alive in this world.

"Can't figure it out?" he said. "They're from Susannah. Susannah Elder. You and your high-and-mighty little friends ruined her life for her all those many years ago. Now she's payin' you back. You pathetic, fucked-up, miserable old bitch, I'm sending you to hell."

I charged through the door just in time to see Boyd Elder snip the oxygen lines and then turn the pair of garden shears toward Hattie Blocker's throat.

Chapter

44

★ ★ ★ ★ ★

"It was a valley very similar to this one," Uncle Tom was telling the children, "but it was thousands of miles away and thousands of years ago."

The ranchers were all seated on benches on the tennis courts, gathered like multitudes around Uncle Tom as he began his story.

"There were two brothers who lived at opposite ends of the valley and they farmed their fields together, growing large crops of grain. One brother had a wife and five children and the other brother was not married and lived alone. Each year at harvest time the two brothers gathered in the grain together from the fields and divided the harvest equally between them."

Marcie and I were sitting on a bench in back and I was fighting to ignore the dull throbbing pain in my left arm. It had been stitched up earlier that evening at Sid Peterson Hospital in Kerrville and it was wrapped in a fashion not dissimilar to that of the mummy of the Pharaoh Esophagus. But that was another of Uncle Tom's stories.

"That night after the first day of harvest," Uncle Tom was saying, "the bachelor brother could not sleep. He lay awake tossing and turning and he thought, 'If God was so good to give me all this grain I should share a little more with my brother, who has a wife and five children to feed.' So in the middle of the night the bachelor brother got up, went to his barn, filled his wheelbarrow full of grain, and wheeled it across the valley where he put the grain in his brother's barn. He did this five more times that night, and then went back to bed and slept peacefully."

"That's more than I'll be doing," I said.

"So tell me what happened," said Marcie.

"You mean you've heard Tom's story?"

"About eighty times."

"Good. Let's hear it again."

"Just about the time the bachelor brother was going to sleep," Uncle Tom continued, "the married brother was tossing and turning and finally he said to his wife, 'You know, God has given us so much we ought to share a bit with my brother. We've got the kids to help us in our old age. He has no one.' And the married brother went to his barn, loaded up his wheelbarrow in the dark, and made a number of trips himself across the valley, depositing each wheelbarrow-load in his brother's barn. Then he went back home and fell into a deep, peaceful sleep.

"In the morning both brothers went out to their barns and each saw that the grain he'd given to his brother had been fully replenished. Each believed that a miracle had occurred, but as they worked together in the fields that day neither felt quite right about mentioning it.

"That night the bachelor brother couldn't sleep. He felt if the Lord had been that good to him he could give his brother half the grain that was in his barn. So he got up, and like the previous night, delivered the grain to his married brother's barn, and then went home to sleep. About that time the married brother was thinking the same thing. He went to his barn, loaded up in the dark, and preceded to make three or four trips across the valley to his brother's barn. Then he, too, went to sleep."

"You'd think with all this video shit today," I said, "this story'd put these kids to sleep, too."

"No way," said Marcie. "They're riveted."

"In the morning both brothers went to their barns and, lo and behold, another miracle had occurred. The barns were just as full as they'd been before each brother had loaded his wheelbarrow. They worked in the fields that day side by side a little uneasy about things, but they didn't say a word to each other about it.

"The third night there was a full moon. The bachelor brother again couldn't sleep. He went to his barn and thought if the Lord could give him this second miracle he could give yet half again of his harvest to his married brother with all of those mouths to feed. He filled up his wheelbarrow and began to trundle it across the valley to his brother's barn.

"At the same time, his brother began tossing and turning and finally decided that if the Lord had given him this second miracle he'd give half again of what he had to his bachelor brother who had no one to look after him. So the married brother went to his barn, loaded up his wheelbarrow, and headed out across the valley.

"It was then, in the middle of the valley, in the moonlight, that the two brothers met. Each was pushing his wheelbarrow of grain to the other one's barn. And as they stood there in the bright moonlight they both realized what had occurred. It was, indeed, a miracle. It was the miracle of brotherly love."

I thought of my own brother, Roger, in Maryland. Married with three kids. We loved each other but we'd become somewhat distant in any number of little ways over the years. We wanted to be in closer touch and we'd both vowed to do something about it, but life often gets in the way. It would be nice if we could just load up our wheelbarrows and head out across the valley.

"There was a mountain overlooking this little valley where the brothers lived," Tom was concluding. "It was not the biggest mountain around, nor was it especially the most beautiful. But there are those who say that the brothers did not go unnoticed. It is said that what happened in the little valley below was the reason God chose Mount Sinai upon which to give Moses the Ten Commandments."

I confess to having had a tear in my eye upon the conclusion of Tom's story. I don't know if it was the story itself or the way Tom had told it. It might've been for my brother, or possibly, for all my brothers. Or maybe it was just the pain in my goddamn arm.

45

★ ★ ★ ★ ★

Later that night, after the kids were in their bunks getting ready to go to sleep, Tom, Marcie, Sambo, and I sat out on the white benches on the tennis courts under the stars. I was giving them a brief rundown, so to speak, of my afternoon at Purple Hills.

". . . so I'm tearing down this hallway shrieking like a wounded faggot—there's blood splattering from my arm all over the wall, giving the whole thing a nice Manson-family ambience—and this totally crazed maniac with a ponytail and a pair of garden shears is ten steps behind me screaming that he's going to send me to hell."

"Sounds unpleasant," said Marcie.

"Sounds like the perfect time to have asked him, 'Why are you following me?' " said Tom.

Sambo, who was quite well attuned to Tom's humor, was smiling like a horse-collar.

"Well, I knew that already," I said, laughing in spite of the rather hideous memory. "Susannah Elder was the girl with no face in the old photograph. Boyd was her son, who the sheriff has since learned was her *illegitimate* son. We also now know that Susannah, as a result of the ensuing scandal, was thrown out of the DRT."

"Just like you were thrown out of the Peace Corps," said Marcie.

" 'De-selected' is the word we like to use. And I got back in and became their fair-haired boy and spent two years in the jungles of Borneo before finally having to be returned to my own culture."

"Let's redirect the conversation back to Susannah," said Marcie.

"Yes, well, she never made it to Borneo. Once you get eighty-sixed from one of these high society–type outfits you *never* get back in. You're lucky if they ever speak to you again. And that's what Boyd Elder claims happened to his mother. She became depressed, alcoholic, suicidal. He remembers strange men visiting his house at all hours when he was a child. When this happened she used to lock him in the closet for hours at a time but he could hear what was going on. He told all this to the sheriff."

"Mama sang bass, Daddy sang tenor," said Marcie. "We had a very dysfunctional family."

"The sheriff wasn't all that sympathetic, either," I said. "After all, the guy's whacked seven little old ladies without blinking an eye."

"But why," said Tom, "did Elder wait over fifty years to exact his revenge?"

"Well, that one's kind of funny," I said. "The sheriff did some checking this afternoon right after Elder was booked.

His mother finally hit the bottom of the lifelong downward spiral that began with her being tossed out of the DRT in disgrace. She finally drank herself to death a little over nine months ago. Just a short time after that, Boyd Elder set out on his campaign of almost biblical vindication."

"So why did he have to wait until his mother died?" said Marcie. "If he'd always felt this way, why didn't he act sooner?"

"I'll tell you what he told the sheriff: 'I don't want Mother to think I'm a bad boy.' "

"That shows a certain degree of thoughtfulness," said Marcie, getting up from the bench. "I've got to check on how the Sunflowers are doing with their marshmallow roast. But congratulations, big brother. I'm glad you caught the bad guy."

After Marcie left I turned to Tom and started to finish the story about my experiences at Purple Hills.

". . . so the guy is gaining on me in the hallway and I can hear his screaming and now I can hear the garden shears clicking and as we thunder past I see two little old ladies standing there and I hear one of them say to the other, 'Oh, look! It's the Senior Olympics!' "

Tom laughed, grabbed both my cheeks with his hands, and gently shook my head in a gesture of love I'd only seen him perform occasionally upon Earl, Roger, Marcie, Sambo (in this case, ears), or anyone else who was lucky enough to be the recipient of his blessing.

"You done good, sonny boy," he said. "Now I've got to go to a meeting with the counselors-in-training down at the dining hall."

"But wait," I said. "Let me tell you what happened when Elder finally caught up with me."

"I can't keep the C.I.T.'s waiting," said Tom, as he walked off the tennis court. "Tell me the rest of it tomorrow."

". . . so anyway," I said to Sam, "I'm on my back at the end of the hallway and Elder's got his knee in my stomach and he's making swooping motions with his hands trying to snip my nose off and I'm just barely holding him back. All of a sudden I see an old man standing in a corner and I shout to him, 'Call the police! Call a nurse! Get help! This guy's trying to kill me!'

"So blood is gushing out of my arm and Elder's eyes are rolling back in his head and the garden shears are snipping, snipping, snipping about an inch away from my nose and the old man—he had a nice, lilting Irish tenor, as I recall—starts singing:

I'm a Yankee Doodle Dandy
A Yankee Doodle do or die
A real live nephew of my Uncle Sam
Born on the Fourth of July!

"Then I hear a tough woman's voice shout, 'Freeze, Elder, or I'll blow your damned head off!'

"Elder froze. So did I.

"Moments later, after Elder was cuffed and taken away, I spoke to the sheriff.

" 'Thanks,' I said gratefully. 'But how the hell did you ever find me here?'

" 'It wasn't too hard,' she said. 'I've had you tailed since you left my office this morning.'

"The old man was still belting it out:

Yankee Doodle went to London
Just to ride the pony
I am that Yankee Doodle Boy!!
I am that Yankee Doodle Bo-y-y-y!!!

" 'Can't you shut him up?' the sheriff said to a nurse.
"The nurse shook her head.
" 'No one's ever been able to,' she said."

I paused, my story over. At that precise moment an armadillo walked by the tennis court and Sam took out after him like an express train. I paced up and down the empty court for a while smoking a cigar. There was no one there, but perhaps because of Tom's story, the valley almost seemed to have a presence in it. It was to that presence that I finally spoke.

"Why do I get the feeling," I said, "that after all these years we're all still playing in the Negro leagues?"

Epilogue

New York City

★ ★ ★ ★ ★

"Four men in an Indian restaurant," I said, two weeks later as I looked around the table. "What are the chances that all of us will lead happy, fulfilling lives?"

"Fucking remote," said Ratso, "if the past is any indicator."

"Or the present," said McGovern.

"Oh, there's always a chance," said Jim Bessman. Jim was a talented freelance writer and possibly the only optimistic vegetarian I'd ever met in my life.

"There's always a chance," I said, "that Ratso will pick up the check."

"I'll drink to that," said McGovern. "In fact I think I'll have a Vodka McGovern." He signaled the tall, turbaned bartender, who bowed and came over to the table. It was a fairly coochi-poochi-boomalini Indian restaurant.

"I'll take a Vodka McGovern," said McGovern.

"A Vodka McGovern," said the bartender smoothly, as if somebody ordered one every night. "And how would you like this Vodka McGovern?"

"Equal portions," said McGovern, "of your best vodka,

just-squeezed orange juice—from Israeli or California oranges, if possible. Israeli oranges are the best in the world—"

"Of course," Ratso and I said in unison. The bartender mumbled something to the waiter in his native dialect.

"—and freshly charged club soda with a squeeze of lime. Just squeeze it, don't bruise it."

The bartender was bowing his way away from the table, but McGovern wasn't quite finished yet.

"In a tall glass," he called after him. "And stirred but not shaken."

The bartender nodded his head gravely. When you're wearing a turban it's hard to nod any other way.

"Stirred but not shaken," said Ratso. "That's the way James Bond orders his drinks."

"Mr. Bond is not known to me," said McGovern.

"Speaking of James Bond," said Jim Bessman, "it's too bad that Rambam couldn't join us tonight."

"Yeah," said Ratso, looking up briefly from his tandoori chicken. "I was kind of hoping Heinrich Himmler could have dropped by as well."

"Saw a guy last night," said McGovern as his Vodka McGovern arrived. "An old man. Looked just like Heinrich Himmler. So I said, 'I don't mean to offend you, but you look just like Heinrich Himmler.' He says, 'I *am* Heinrich Himmler. I've been living in Westchester for forty years and now I'm back and I'm gonna kill six million more Jews and three NFL players.' 'Who're the three NFL players?' I asked him. He says, 'You see! Der Führer was right! Nobody cares about the Jews!' "

"Nobody cares about the Irish, either," said Ratso.

"Now that we've got *that* settled," said Bessman, "where *is* Rambam?"

"He's in Lopbouri, Thailand," I said. "Jumping."

"Jumping?" said McGovern. "Why can't he jump right here in New York?"

"I can think of a few places he could jump *off*," said Ratso, "and at least one he could jump *up*."

"Not with the Royal Thai Paratroopers," I said.

★

There is a tasty pistachio ice cream dessert that many Indian restaurants feature. It is called *kulfi*. Unfortunately, "kulfi" is also the way most Indians pronounce the word "coffee." This can sometimes make for a long, not to mention tedious, evening.

"I'll have some *kulfi*," said Ratso to the waiter.

"One *kulfi*," he said.

"I'll just have some coffee," I said.

"One kulfi," he said.

"You want coffee?" I asked Bessman.

"I don't drink coffee," said Bessman, "but I'll try some *kulfi*."

"Two *kulfis*, one kulfi," said the waiter.

"I'll try the *kulfi*," said McGovern, with a hearty Irish laugh that somewhat overwhelmed the subliminal sitar music.

"You want kulfi?"

"Yes. To go with the *kulfi*."

"Okay," said the waiter, "that's three *kulfis* and two kulfis."

"Maybe I won't have that *kulfi*," said Ratso. "I'm watching my diet. But I will have some coffee."

"Okay," said the waiter, "that's two *kulfis* and three kulfis."

"You know," said Ratso after the waiter had gone away, "maybe I should've ordered decaf."

★

Later that night, in the light rain, Ratso bummed a cigar, and we walked through the Village together. Waiting to cross Sixth Avenue, I took out of my coat pocket a letter I'd received from the beekeeper and, shielding it from the rain with my cowboy hat, showed it to Ratso. He read it carefully, puffing on the cigar and shaking his head several times in some untitled emotion.

"Poignant, Kinkstah," he said. "Poignant. The guy lives such a fragile and isolated life to begin with and then he loses his bees and he's all alone. It's hard to believe people like this really can and do exist in the world."

He handed me the letter. I folded it and put it back in my pocket. We crossed the street against the traffic and the rain.

"Try four men in an Indian restaurant," I said.

★

"Start talkin'," I said, as I picked up the blower on the left. It was later that night sometime after Cinderella's curfew and I'd been looking through a copy of *Cowpokes*, a collection of work by the World's Greatest Cowboy Cartoonist, Ace Reid.

"Hill Country update," said a familiar voice. It was Marcie calling from Texas.

"Spit it," I said, as I let my mind wander vaguely back to the ranch. I was smoking a cigar and some of the smoke drifted lazily over the cat as she slept under the desk lamp. She didn't seem to mind.

"According to the Kerrville papers," said Marcie, "Boyd Elder's looking at life."

"So am I," I said.

"It's really sick," Marcie continued. "He's starting to get marriage proposals and movie offers."

"That's more than I can say for myself."

"Then there's the news about Pam and Sam."

"Don't tell me they ran off together?"

"No. Pam is engaged to Wayne the wrangler."

"Hell, if I sat around every night watching ceramic leaf ash-trays glaze in a kiln I'd probably be engaged to Wayne the wrangler." I thought very fleetingly of Pam Stoner standing outside the green trailer in the moonlight. Where did summer romances go for the winter?

"What's the matter with Sam?" I said.

"Well, there's nothing really the *matter* with Sam," said Marcie. "It's just that he seems to have developed a rather un-pleasant new habit. He's started to spend an inordinate amount of his time rolling around in horse manure."

"When did you first notice this behavior?" I said.

"About a week ago when Sam walked into the house and the whole place has smelled like horseshit ever since."

"I see."

"You see," said Marcie, "but you don't smell."

"Well, it's just a suggestion," I said, "but how about this possibility. Sam stays in the lodge and assumes responsibility for conducting ranch business from there. You know, closes up the place for the winter, mails out statements to parents. In the meantime Tom moves down to your white trailer and you move over to my green trailer. I don't know. It's just an idea."

"We'll take it under review," said Marcie. "In the meantime, *why* do you think Sam is doing this? Is his inner child reaching out through such primitive behavior to express its rage and anger at his traumatic, dysfunctional early background? Do you think *that* could be it?"

"Hardly," I said, just as Doc Phelps had replied when I suggested that the coast of California was as far away as you could run. "Hardly."

"You ask me why Sam is rolling in the horse manure?" I continued.

"Yes, O great Chief Fuckbrain."

"The answer is very simple. To paraphrase old Slim: 'He wants to see the world.' "

"You would've made a great philosopher, brother dear," said Marcie. "Or at least an assistant professor at one of the larger Southern party schools. By the way, Pat Knox called for your address. She says she's sending you a homemade fruit-cake."

"What does she mean by that?" I said.

★

Several hours later I'd just sailed into a peaceful dream riding upon the back of Dr. Doolittle's giant pink sea snail. Into the dream came the unwelcome sound of a Japanese gardener with one of those leaf-blowing devices and I realized the blower by the bed was ringing. I collared the blower and heard a high-pitched, ridiculous, agitated voice.

"Help me!! Help me!!" screamed the faintly familiar macaw-like tones. "Help me!! There's a giant swarm of bees right outside my window!!"

"Ratso, you nerd—" I said, but the line had been disconnected.

The cat yawned mightily and went back to sleep. I got up and walked over to the kitchen window and looked down at Vandam Street. I thought of what George Christy, the columnist for the *Hollywood Reporter*, had once told me. Years ago Christy had been in a cab with Truman Capote on their way to a Peggy Lee concert. Capote was wearily watching the streets flash by and then he turned to Christy and said, "You know, George, the more I see of life the more I know there are only 150 of us in this world."

I looked up at the sky and there were about a million stars. A million stars for 150 people. Good odds, I thought, but a slow track.

Suddenly, it's Hoedown Night at Echo Hill and the same stars are looking down on music and dancing and bales of hay and saddles scattered across the old tennis court; and there are pigtails and ponytails and counselors with packs of non-filter cigarettes rolled up in the sleeves of their T-shirts; and Uncle Tom and Aunt Min are all dressed up in their western clothes and smiling, Uncle Floyd is smoking his cigar, and Slim Dodson is serving up glazed donuts and apple juice; Doc and Hilda Phelps are standing by, stately in their Navajo finery; Dot is clapping her hands to the music and shouting encouragement from the shadows; Earl Buckelew comes riding over on horseback and our neighbor Cabbie is watching from his Jeep with his old dog Rip; and Aunt Joan is teaching the smallest girls a dance.

They stand in a line facing Aunt Joan with their arms around one another's waists, tragically fragile, impossibly young. And the stars shine down and they dance beneath the constellation of my childhood.

> *There were ten pretty girls*
> *in the village school*
> *There were ten pretty girls*
> *in the village school*
> *Some were short, some were tall*
> *and the boy loved them all*
> *But you can't marry ten pretty girls.*
>
> *Five were blondes and four brunettes*
> *and one was a saucy little redhead*
> *The girls grew up, the boy left school*
> *And in '39 he married—*
> *the saucy little redhead.*

As dawn hustled the stars out of the Manhattan sky I was still sitting at my desk holding the letter from the beekeeper.

> *Dear Kinky,*
> *As you've probably guessed I'm not one for writing letters. I just wanted you to know that I'm sorry I*

hung you out to dry that day. I also wanted to thank you. I've heard that the sheriff saved your life but I believe it was you who saved mine. There's not a lot of people who'd give a damn about saving my life. I'm the kind of person most people call a character or maybe a loner or maybe worse. But I'm really a man who's seen the world and knows that he never wants to be a part of it.

I'm sad to say my bees have never returned. They cannot really be replaced. It may sound funny to most people but I've lived by myself all my life and the bees were like friends and family to me. Now I am truly alone in this place. I'm thinking of going to Africa as a mercenary or going to Hawaii and raise orchids. If you ever go to one of those places, I hope you'll try to look me up. If you can find me.

Your friend,
Willis Hoover

P.S.: Small world department—Hattie Blocker died in her sleep last night. My mama's now the last surviving debutante.

Acknowledgments

★ ★ ★ ★ ★

The author would like to thank the following Americans: Don Imus, longtime imaginary childhood friend and toboggan companion, for his continuing encouragement and support, up to and including plugging *Elvis, Jesus & Coca-Cola* from the intensive care unit of New York Hospital; Mike McGovern, my favorite Irish poet, who, over dim sum in Chinatown one morning, came up with the title *Armadillos & Old Lace*; Chuck Adams, my discerning and dedicated editor, and Joann DiGenarro, Maya Rutherford, and all the folks at Simon & Schuster for believing in me and working to help me achieve my personal goals of becoming fat, famous, and financially fixed by fifty; Esther "Lobster" Newburg, my literary agent, for repeatedly telling people, many of whom already disliked me intensely, that I was a genius; Elisa Petrini, who survived being my editor once and, God love her, is my editor again for *Elvis, Jesus & Coca Cola* in paperback (Bantam); and Jim Landis, Jane Meara, and Lori Ames, whom I'm no longer "with," as they say, but to whom I'm forever grateful for so generously helping me on my way.

Also, a tip of the ol' cowboy hat to Steve Rambam, long-suffering technical advisor; Jay Wise; Max Swafford; the drop-dead gorgeous Stephanie DuPont for petulantly sitting this one out; Dennis Laviage, for supplying the Jesus joke on page 11; and, last but not least, Rudyard Kipling, for providing the particularly apt similes for the three occasions in which Sambo the dog smiles. May Rudyard continue to inspire and Sambo continue to smile.

P.S.: I'd like to thank two fine ladies, both good Americans and good sports, for their help and indulgence in this obvious work of fiction: Frances A. Kaiser, Sheriff, Kerr County; and the Hon. Patricia E. Knox, Justice of the Peace, Precinct 1, Kerrville, Texas.